WHEN YOU RETURN

Isabella Ayubi

Dedications

For my parents, who taught me what real love looks like.
Thank you for everything.

Prologue

A Prince of the Gate changed his features as easily as one would don a new coat. He fashioned his hair to be shorter, shorn close to his neck. The harsh angles of his face were softened, and the tone of his skin deepened to the point that one would never know he spent so little time in the sun. The transformation always started out subtle, with gradual changes to things such as the pitch of his voice and gait. The only part of him that could not be changed were his eyes.

No, a Prince of the Gate could never change his eyes.

The Murmur

*E*very once in a while, fate picks its favorites. I'm still not quite sure why it picked us. Her, I can understand. Me? Less so.

Still, I'll never forget the day I first laid eyes on her. She was stunning; a golden ray of light from the highest heavens, a beauty that refreshed the senses as a light spring rain revives the earth. An absolute angel.

Or so I thought, until she held a sizable shard of broken glass to my throat, and the daydream shattered. What a lovely few seconds.

Chapter One

Walking the Fine Line

"Can we talk this out?" Keir feared that moving even an inch forward would inevitably result in his throat being pierced. He wasn't in the mood to crumble into a cloaked heap this night.

"State your business." Her voice did not match her soft features. It sounded as if suspicion and annoyance had collided to create the same gravel that lay scattered underneath their scuffed boots.

Keir's dark eyebrows flicked up. "Excuse me?"

She scoffed, and the shadows that were cast from the nearby flickering light post carved hollows into her cheeks, accentuating the sharp line of her mouth and the annoyed set of her honey-brown eyes.

"Don't play smart. I know your kind." With that, she pressed the dingy glass a touch further toward his throat.

"My kind?" Keir's voice turned mocking, although in hindsight that was a poor choice as the jagged fragment pricked through his skin.

"Curfew has been instated for non-citizens. And you're dangerously close to the Gate."

Keir then noted that her focus did not stray from his eyes, completely disregarding his hands. *First mistake.* His hands swiftly came up to shove her away, causing her to stumble several steps as her center of gravity slipped out from under her. She lost her hold on the neck of the broken bottle, and gravel splashed around her hands as she tried to break her fall. The softest yelp he'd ever heard left her lips, but she clamped down on the sound, small as it was, and glared at him. The look that she gave was sharper than the shattered glass had ever been.

"Now that we have breathing room, if you can guarantee that I won't die by a drunk's bottle, we can talk like civilized people." Keir extended his hand to her.

The girl looked at his hand suspiciously. Perhaps she wondered if he could sprout knives from his fingers to slash her with, and she made no move to reach for it. She pushed herself to her feet and dusted herself off with one hand, all the while watching Keir with wary eyes. Her lips were still pursed the same way they had been a moment earlier.

Keir straightened and withdrew his offer, readjusting the wooden clasp of his worn cloak.

"I was not aware of a curfew," he replied, "I've been away from Thulta for some time."

"Still doesn't explain why I *saw* you at the Gate." She countered, "I-"

"Dilly-Dally, what are you doing?" A group of three men rounded the corner. The tallest one looked between them and laughed loudly.

"Tell me you weren't trying to arrest *him*."

She cleared her throat uncomfortably. "Trevor, you don't understand, I saw him leaving the Gate."

Trevor shook his head, "You could see a duck fly over and try to cuff it." The other two men snickered at that, and something in Keir felt strangely uncomfortable.

"Sorry Keir. She's... new." The shorter one of the group stated.

She whirled around. "Ben, I am not! And how do you know his name?" She jerked a thumb in Keir's direction.

"Oh, Dilly. He's a stone mason, we've seen him on and off for the past year." Trevor chuckled and then clapped her on the back as he turned to leave, the sound echoing through the alleyway. "Nice try though."

Her shoulders drooped. A subtle movement, but Keir caught onto it, nonetheless.

"Sentries, right?"

"At your service." Trevor nodded and then looked to, '*Dilly.*'

"Come on, you can tag-along to the Tap if you can tone down that 'intuition' of yours." Trevor laughed again and tipped his hat to Keir. "Good evening."

Keir returned the nod, and a strange feeling prickled at the corner of his mind as he watched how quickly her countenance changed. Any trace of disappointment from being mistaken had been wiped from her features and she stood taller again with a newfound determination.

"My apologies, sir." She flexed the hand that hung limply by her side and turned on her heel to follow the other Sentries.

What a strange way to start the evening, Keir thought.

And even stranger, was his sudden craving for a refreshment at the Tap.

The Tap was a bustling tavern that aspired to be a restaurant and a gambling hall in one. Tonight, rowdiness and cacophony filled the air. No one paid any mind to the cloaked man that took a seat in the corner, wedged between the wall and the oak counter. Except one girl, who sat sandwiched between two friends who howled at jokes told at her expense. She smiled too. Tonight should be a night for laughter, not grudges. Although she wished that she wore her smile as genuinely as it appeared to anyone watching.

When the conversation at her table started to take a turn as her friends kept guzzling their pungent drinks, she shimmied out of her seat. All the stale air offended her headache. Perhaps she could find a seat near the counter where it appeared less populated and maybe formally apologize in the process.

"Mind if I sit?" She asked him, gesturing towards the stool.

Keir lifted his glass from his side and wiped the condensation away with his sleeve. "Only if my throat won't be in danger."

She hopped up and took a breath, "I'm sorry about that, by the way."

Keir looked over his shoulder, to the others in her group and then his gaze returned to her.

"It's fine, you were doing your job, no?" The lantern hanging above the counter struck his eyes with light, and she noted what a peculiar shade of caramel they were. Almost as if they could shine on their own without external light. She wondered if her own dark eyes had ever looked that way.

"Trying to, at least." She shrugged one shoulder and dug her fingernail into a groove in the table.

"Always trust your gut, even if people laugh at you." He said, and then paused before continuing.

"Do they always do that?" Keir questioned, and she knew he referred to the others.

"Do what?"

"Laugh at you." A simple question, but a part of her felt surprised that he had caught on to that, instead of reprimanding her for a mistake.

"Oh. Sometimes, but humor is cleansing for the soul, right? I can take a joke." Another shrug, and she drummed her fingers on her arm.

Keir fell quiet for a moment, then he took a sip from his cup and set it down. "Do you have a name or did your parents truly christen you, 'Dilly-Dally'."

She made a face but quickly corrected it. "I named myself, but not... that. It's Idalia."

"Idalia." He repeated, "I'm Keir, nice to meet you. I have decided to abandon the memory of our first meeting and never speak of it again." He offered his hand and smiled.

"I'd... appreciate that actually." She shook his hand and then her eyes snagged on a deck of abandoned playing cards near her elbow.

"When you said I should trust my gut, it sounded like a smart idea, but we both see where that got me tonight." She took the cards and began to shuffle.

This time Keir shrugged, "I don't know, I'd prefer to have a Sentry who relied on instinct rather than one who never looked into anything too closely."

"Then I guess it's good news for you that you're not a criminal." She chuckled and dealt an equal number of cards between them.

Keir laughed and she paused her dealing. "Wait, are you?"

He shook his head, "What kind of criminal would I be if I told you?"

"A very imprisoned one."

He just smiled. She had never been a betting woman, but she would have put money down that there was more than just mischief lingering behind those eyes.

She didn't get to ponder that long because he asked, "Did you always want to be a guard?"

She slid his cards toward him and picked up her own. "I always knew I wanted to make a difference. I don't want to be remembered for some great big thing but-" She discarded a four of spades. "I would like to make a few people's lives better at least. And safer, typically means better."

Keir laid a suit down. "That's very... noble of you." He nodded his approval.

"What about you? Always wanted to be in masonry?" She plucked a card from the pile.

"It's honest work."

"Doesn't sound like your dream job." She replied, amused.

Keir laid down a set of aces, "It's the closest I can get. Besides, I prefer working with my hands rather than working with paper." A chuckle left him, and he propped his arm up on the counter.

"Okay then, what is your dream job?"

"So many questions." He clicked his tongue, "Let's shift the focus back to you." He laughed again. *He had a strong but gentle laugh.*

Idalia deposited the final card of her hand. "Evading a Sentries' questioning, I could have you sent through the Gate for that."

"Oh dear, let's both stay out of there, yes?" He said in jest, although she thought that she caught a shadow glaze over his eyes for a split moment. More than likely, the shifting light of the lantern on him could be blamed.

"Dilly-Dally, time... to go..." Trevor appeared beside her chair, leaning heavily on her side. While Idalia did not possess a frail frame, his much larger body obviously expended more weight.

"You are drunk out of your mind." She shoved his top-heavy self backwards and moved from her stool.

"Hey, do you want help getting them back to the compound?" Keir set his cards down.

"No, it's fine. I've got a system at this point." She slung Trevor's arm around her shoulders to distribute his weight more evenly. "Thank you though." Idalia tacked on.

"Of course." Keir stood from his stool as well. If the other man stumbled, he would much rather be the one to catch him than have all his weight crush Idalia.

"Playin' cards without me?" Trevor pouted as he looked at their interrupted game through glazed eyes.

"Come on. Mox and Ben already started back." She gave him a moment to find his footing.

"I'll be waiting to finish this game of ours sometime." Keir gave her a smile, but something in his expression held difficult for her to place. He had given her that impression quite a few times tonight.

"I'll bring the broken bottles." She returned the smile and with that, both her and Trevor left the Tap.

Keir felt a spark of amusement at her words, but that amusement was quickly doused when he caught himself staring at the doorway long after she left.

When he left the Tap that night, Keir had two things that relentlessly circulated in his mind.

Those Sentries took Idalia's intuition for granted and he thanked his lucky stars that she hadn't trusted those instincts tonight.

Chapter Two
The Side She Chose

T he sandy gravel indented Idalia's palms as she flipped backwards to avoid becoming a resting place for Trevor's sword as it swung through the air.

"A little sloppy." Trevor dug his boot into the gravel before he pounced.

As she dodged him, Idalia's waist-length braid smacked her shoulder like a whip. "I'm still in one piece, I'd call that smart."

"But what if there's no room to back-flip, Dilly?"

"Then I'd do this." Her lips pulled back from her teeth as the sun ricocheted from her blade to Trevor's eyes, temporarily blinding her training partner.

"Hey!" He complained, right before Idalia kicked her leg against the back of his knees, and Trevor lurched to the ground. "You won't be able to use that trick on night rounds." He grumbled and glared at Idalia through stray wisps of tawny hair. Idalia thrust her hand forward to pull him to his feet.

"But it's wildly effective during the day."

Trevor shook his head, "Be serious, Idalia. You should practice maneuvers that apply anytime." Trevor readjusted his hand placement on the handle of his sword, beckoning Idalia to get back into position.

"Different situations call for different approaches," Idalia reasoned as she raised her blade pointedly towards her fellow Sentry.

Trevor sighed as they launched into their second round of sword-fighting that afternoon. Sparks bounced from their steel. The unwavering Thultan sun combined with their rapid movements made Idalia long to feel the caress of the ocean breeze.

Trevor just narrowly avoided a slice to his ear as the back door to the Sentry compound slammed open on its squeaking hinges. "Trevor, I need you for a debriefing." Mox motioned towards the inside and Trevor tossed his weapon haphazardly in the corner. Mox was their leader, and he reported directly to King Damien and Queen Anastasia of Thulta. The royal family had kept watch over this land for generations, and it was the Sentries' task to carry out all orders demanded of them. From there, the commands would transfer to Trevor as Mox's right hand, and then each member of their unit would follow through accordingly. Idalia fell under the lower rung of their Sentry hierarchy, but she was determined that with enough hard work she could climb the ranks.

"We'll stop for today." He declared, and stalked off into the compound, leaving Idalia alone in the small courtyard.

She deposited her own blade and brushed the tan-colored dust from her knees before she slipped out onto the main road. Idalia's lungs welcomed the reprieve as her boots thumped against the wooden boardwalk that connected the rows of brightly colored shops. She wasn't technically on duty yet but Idalia believed that if the situation arose, it was always a good idea to have at least one person keeping an eye on things.

Of course, it was quite easy to become distracted by the bustle and lively chatter that filtered through Thulta in tandem with the birdsong and squealing of mischievous children. Idalia smiled as she watched a peddler hand a little boy no older than nine a paper cone with a mountain of white spun sugar on top. She had been around that age when she made the decision to become a guard. Idalia would watch from the balcony of the orphanage that she called home for the formative years of her life as groups of Sentries patrolled the streets. She'd always thought them so brave, and she wanted a chance to fight for others in the same way that those Sentries did. So, she trained each day until she joined their ranks at eighteen. Each round that she completed felt like another chance to prove her usefulness to her fellow guards. She jumped at any opportunity that allowed her to show how worthy she was to protect Thulta.

Idalia loved her home, and all its perfect imperfections. The places where the cobblestone paths accumulated leaves and moss from the spring rains made her think of a road that could lead to a fantastical cottage in the woods. Where the paint faded from the façade of a building, Idalia saw the charm of the exposed brick underneath.

The Thultans' that were fortunate enough to live towards the south, built their homes with windows that offered a glimpse of the sea in its beckoning mystery. The Sentry compound that Idalia lived in did not have the luxury of such a beautiful view. So, Idalia simply enjoyed gazing up and watching others' multi-colored drapes billow and dance in the wind as to a peaceful symphony. If one were to trail their gaze to the east, then they would look upon the magnanimous pristine castle perched high on a cliff. It was like a beacon of white marble, a glorious structure that represented a common desire of all Thultans. *Strength, unity, goodness.*

Thulta in its own right was a beautiful place during the day. But there was a quiet solace to her city when the sun fell, and the moon and stars took command of the sky. However, many mistake the peace of night for the sound of safety. Nightfall lures those who do not belong amongst the color and light of Thulta like a siren's call. Idalia's fingers found purchase on the rungs of a metal ladder as she pulled herself up to the flat roof of a canary-yellow shop. Sometimes, Idalia could swear that she could see for miles from this ledge. Her gaze would always wander beyond where any innocent eyes should linger as she watched the Gate. It was as if an entirely different world began with the first iron stake. The brightness and life that seemed to exude from Thulta abruptly trailed off when any soul neared the Gate. It was the home to every morally gray criminal that ever dared to poison the light of Thulta with their misdeeds.

On many occasions, Idalia stood face-to-face with the structure as they handed over captives to the Gate guards. Her stomach would twist as her mind recollected the horror stories told about those within, especially regarding the two rulers that governed the Gate's wretched throne. It was a miserable place to live if one didn't hold a high political position. Those that paid little mind to the corruption that seeped into the very streets where their citizens resided seemed to have no qualms with their homeland. At one point in time, a treaty of sorts had been constructed between the past royalty of Thulta and the old Gate King. The land that belonged to the Gate had a different name as well, *Rayavin*. As the years went by, that name faded away and was rarely used. The treaty allowed for both lands to benefit from the other. The Thultans' would be free of corruption and malicious intent, and the Princes would be generously compensated for each prisoner that the Sentries sent through. Idalia's thoughts shattered as a scream tore through the alleyway beneath her.

Chapter Three
What She Was Made For

"Help!" A woman's high-pitched shriek of terror was instantly muffled by the clamping of a hand over her mouth. "Mmphmm!" The woman screamed with all her might as she thrashed against her captor's hold.

Idalia's fingers instinctively curved as she grasped the dagger at her waist and unsheathed it within seconds. A large man dressed in dark gray had the woman pinned against him as his other hand aggressively fished around the coin purse at her hip, spilling most of its contents.

"Hey!" Idalia barked, swinging down from the ladder before her feet connected with the ground. "Let go of her."

The man barely paid Idalia any heed as he stuffed several stolen coins into his pocket. Idalia advanced with her dagger raised, and finally, the robber looked in her direction, "Go away, girl, This doesn't concern you."

"Mmphm!" His captive squirmed and begged Idalia to stay with wide, fearful eyes.

"Step away from her." Idalia warned, and the man yanked the woman's purse off of her shoulder, snapping the leather strap in two.

"Put that little butter knife away before you hurt yourself," the man grumbled. He tightened his grip over the woman's face, who would surely be sporting bruises on her cheeks. A shaft of sunlight fell over Idalia's shoulder as she moved towards the robber, highlighting the design of a crimson hibiscus with a sword-like stem that was stitched on her uniform. His eyes shot to the logo, then to Idalia as realization twisted his features into an unpleasant expression. "Sentry."

"Miss, on three I'm going to need you to throw your head back." Idalia said steadily and cast a pointed look to another area of the robber's body while the man was distracted by his victim. "One." Idalia took a step forward, "Two." The sunlight gleamed off of her small blade. "Three."

The woman slammed the heel of her fashionable boot onto the instep of the robber's foot. The man let out a grunt of pain as he fell to his knees and released her long enough for Idalia to make her move. Idalia grabbed the broken purse strap and yanked the man's arms forward as she quickly tied the makeshift cord around his wrists. "I didn't even need my 'butter knife.'" She said facetiously. Idalia made sure that his restraints were secured tightly before she cast a look over her shoulder to the other lady.

"Your coins are in his left coat pocket, although I'm going to need to borrow this." Idalia tugged on the strap for emphasis and the man grunted in discomfort and frustration.

The girl wrung her hands frantically, "Oh, please keep it, thank you." She scrambled to retrieve her money and cast a grateful look toward Idalia before scurrying away.

"I wasn't going to harm her-"

"Assaulted robbery is unlawful, regardless of your intentions."

"You don't understand! My family-" His words poured out in a rush, so at odds with his rude demeanor a mere few moments before.

"Got another one for the Gate?" A voice sounded behind them, and Idalia turned to see Ben stroll down the alleyway. "What kind of makeshift knot is that?" Ben chuckled and hauled the man to his feet by his collar.

"I improvised." Idalia released her grip on the strip of leather, and Ben ushered the man forward with a less than gentle push to his back.

"Well I guess if it works, it works."

Idalia slipped her dagger back into its sheath as Ben added, "We're sending some over tonight, we can group him in with the rest."

The man's eyes widened in horror, "No! Please, I'm sorry, don't send me there." He tried to cement his heels into the cobblestone, but it was to no avail as Ben roughly pushed him forward. "I have a family!"

"Should have thought of that beforehand, mister." Ben gave Idalia a look that conveyed: *Can you believe the audacity of this guy?*

"Please." The robber begged, turning hopeless eyes to Idalia. Perhaps he believed that he could glean some mercy from her simply because she was female. It was a wide assumption that some women were more apt to have bleeding hearts. While she did try to keep everyone's best interests in mind, Idalia also had a responsibility. So, she trained her gaze forward and did her best to block out the protesting cries of the robber she had apprehended. No one wanted to cross the Gate, no matter what they had done.

It was common knowledge that if you go in, you're not coming out.

Chapter Four
A Deathly Risk

Idalia had gone through the same scheduled routine this past week. With the monotonous training sessions and unchanged faces, she couldn't stop herself from thinking that there had to be more that she could do to make a difference.

Maybe she shouldn't complain about peace in the city. Any other guard would be delighted at the prospect of less work and physical exertion. She wanted her hunches to be right sometimes... or even acknowledged.

"Trevor I was thinking, maybe we should rotate-" She started, but her words were interrupted.

"Not now, Idalia." Trevor brushed by her and slipped into the meeting room. Something must have been wrong for him to use her actual name. Perhaps she shouldn't have wished so strongly for action.

She wrapped her fingers around the metal doorknob and gave it a tug to follow him. *Locked*. Something in her stomach sank, as if she'd swallowed rocks and fallen into the ocean. This wasn't the first time they had kept her out of a serious discussion. She stood just as capable and trained as the rest. Idalia pressed her ear to the crack in the door to eavesdrop. Their voices were low and murmuring, but she was able to decipher the conversation for the most part.

"Is there any real proof to substantiate these rumors?" She heard Trevor inquire.

"Our sources say yes." Someone else replied.

"That would ruin us."

"The Thultans' have become so soft that they've grown weak. Our unit isn't large enough to combat the sheer amount of monsters that could come pouring out." Mox's voice was laced with a grumble. "We need to find an advantage."

A war? Something in Idalia's chest seized.

"It's suicide to cross." She heard Trevor's voice again.

"And even if by some miracle, the Princes spare our lives long enough for us to figure out their plans, we could be dead before we have a chance to act."

The Princes. A war. Things were clicking into place.

"We have to do something," Ben chimed in. "There has to be some way to appeal to them or some way to trick them."

Trevor laughed incredulously, "Both are sharp as a tack! Please, pray tell, how you plan on coercing them to willingly divulge their secrets."

Idalia heard another Sentry that she didn't know that well utter, "What is a weakness that all men share?"

"Money?"

"Power?" Came a second reply.

She heard the muffled sound of a table being smacked with a frustrated hand. "No, you idiots. A pretty girl."

A silence settled in the room, and Idalia had a sinking suspicion that she knew what they were eluding to. *The only female Sentry they had stood pressed outside this door.*

"Okay let me just get this straight. Our plan is to send her through, hope that she doesn't lose her head while trying to seduce one of them and trust that she makes it out before chaos breaks loose?" Idalia could practically see Trevor pinching the bridge of his nose as he spoke.

Another scattered silence.

"If that doesn't work, we'll come up with something else. She is the most expendable. Whether they kill or keep her, we can still function." Mox added.

During Idalia's childhood, she got her hand caught in a thornbush that grew outside of the orphanage. It clung and bit into her skin until it drew blood. That's what she felt like now, except instead of her hand, her heart was quickly becoming entangled with the thorned vines of those words.

No, she was not expendable. She had value. She *added* value to this team. She would prove it. Through whatever means were necessary she would complete the mission and divert this war. Even if it meant losing herself in the process.

"Go get her." She heard Mox say.

Idalia pushed off the door and sped down the hallway before the door clicked open. She didn't want them to know that she had heard everything.

"Dilly-Dally? Where are you?" The familiar sound of Trevor's heavy footfalls filled her ears, and she turned the corner again nonchalantly.

"What's wrong?" She questioned, knowing full well what he would ask of her.

"Come with me." He jerked his chin to an empty planning hall, and she followed him in.

"We've talked it through, and we need you to head up a very dangerous mission." Trevor said carefully. Idalia hated that he could lie so blatantly through his teeth. Perhaps this is what she would have to become for this task. A perfect liar.

"Oh? What for?"

"We think that the Princes are going to open the Gate and start a war with Thulta." Trevor sank into a chair.

She did not have to feign her concern on this topic, she felt the apprehension in every bone. "Information extraction?"

Trevor nodded, "Do whatever you have to do. Get as close as you can to one of the Princes or someone they trust."

Idalia pulled her hair back behind her neck, "It won't be easy, and how do I get inside in the first place?"

Trevor shrugged in an apparent attempt to buy time to formulate an idea. "We'll place a charge on you. This way, you can enter under the guise of a criminal."

"What if they kill me before I can even get close to them?" She reasoned. She wasn't looking for a way out, but searching for a way to eventually leave with all her limbs still attached.

Trevor hesitated, "Play your cards right. Be smart."

That wasn't the helpful advice she had hoped for. Perhaps she would be more on her own than she thought. Trevor stood from his chair and headed for the door. Before he turned to exit, Idalia spoke, "Why...did you lock me out of that meeting?"

He paused with his hand on the doorknob. "Didn't think it was necessary for you to be there, Dilly-Dally."

She swallowed and pushed open the other door. "I would have preferred to be there when you all made the decision to send me into the vipers pit."

Chapter Five
Don't Fret, It's Only Death

Idalia dug her fingernails into her thighs as she listened to the other Sentries formulate a more detailed plan. Along with their rambling, she crafted a mental list of her own.

1. Do not draw too much attention, unless necessary to capture the interest of one of the Princes.

2. Be wary of what she repeats in their presence.

3. Memorize everything spoken that could give the Sentries an advantage.

4. Every week, find a way to leave undetected in order to deposit a coded letter containing a report of any information collected. She was to wedge the envelope underneath a loose stone by the southwest corner of the Gate.

5. Use whatever method necessary to secure the trust of one Prince. Both would be too risky.

And while the others did not add this note, she made sure to jot down one more thing for herself:

6. Try not to die.

Chapter Six
Unsaid Farewells

The day that Idalia faced her fate by crossing over into the Princes domain had a heavy sense to it. It wasn't fear that clouded the dwindling hours, but the fact that not one person seemed sad to see her go. The same routine. Everything, just as it always had been.

It wouldn't matter, she supposed, if she didn't make it back. They might come up with another plan, but at that point a war could be underway and this beautiful kingdom she so desperately wanted to protect would be trampled and overrun.

They had certainly helped her look the part. Trevor looked ever the annoyed guard at having to escort Idalia through the Gate. The Sentries had bound her wrists beforehand in the hope that loose binding would prevent her from being rendered defenseless. It always made a shiver trail down her spine when she saw the Gate, like drops of icy water rolling down her back and freezing on her skin. The Gate itself was a massive, ink-black, wrought iron structure that spanned as far as the eye could see. Along with the swirls and designs, the Gate brandished spikes atop the bars that could pierce through bone. No one dared to approach and for good reason.

Everything looked dead, from what she could tell. It looked as if a wildfire had taken its time in ravaging the landscape, leaving nothing but a blanket of charred ground and rotting trees. Idalia wondered how anyone survived here, if they did at all. When the Gate opened, it did not screech or groan. *It must be maintained well.*

One may believe that the Gate was the most daunting symbol of this dark place, but the castle that lay within was just as wretched in its opulence. Foreboding blackstone walls climbed skywards, and the spike-endowed parapets seemed to graze the clouds with metal claws. Vines of poisonous ivy crawled over the curving faces of the castle. It was as if the ivy could absorb the darkness within to spread into each crevice of the blackened brick. From her position on the ground, Idalia could see wrought iron bars encasing the windows that were visible. *These villains must revel in their appearances,* Idalia thought. Because this castle was less something from a fairytale, and more the inspiration of any horror story that had to do with shadows.

Trevor relinquished Idalia to one of the Gate guards, and he promptly returned to the safe side of their world. No words of comfort, no well wishes uttered. Idalia nodded her goodbyes and watched as the only friends she had, left her to a possible death-sentence.

She could do this. She could prove to everyone that she could be someone worth missing. That she deserved to be treated the same as the rest. She, their equal. When she succeeded, they would never laugh at her again.

Chapter Seven
A Mistake of Permanence

A guard coated in sable obsidian armor tossed Idalia in front of the two Princes as if she weighed no more than a stuffed doll. "This one was dropped at the north Gate." The large man growled. One Prince reclined back on his throne. His lavish seat consisted of heavy, burnished gold and iron architecture. The spikes resembled those on top of the Gate at its crown. The Prince drummed his fingers on the carved armrest. A woman in a deep silver gown and burgundy lipstick ran her hand over his sleeve as she perched on a blood-red chaise next to him.

"Thief, I presume?" He asked, amused. Idalia did not turn her attention to him, however. Her gaze stayed stuck on his brother who stood unaccompanied on the right-hand side of the steps. Something about him felt familiar, but for the life of her she couldn't figure out why.

"You would do well to answer." The first Prince mused, although she still offered no response.

"Perhaps she's mute?" The woman beside the first Prince laughed, and it was a startingly sinister sound. One of the guard's dirty boots made contact with Idalia's leg. In the same manner that one would nudge an animal's body to see if it was alive or not.

"Don't touch me." Idalia grit out as she tore her eyes away from the standing Prince to glare at the guard.

"She does speak." The Prince on the throne surveyed Idalia. "Who escorted you here?"

"Some Sentry." She dared another quick glance to his brother but then her eyes settled on the other woman's shoes. Small, metallic, silver serpents laced up her ankles and Idalia could only assume that the design carried around to the heels of her stilettos.

"I assumed as much, no one crosses over of their own volition unless they're drunk or incredibly daft." He commented, which made the female beside him laugh as she sipped a dark liquid from her frosty glass.

"She doesn't look intoxicated." She scanned Idalia on the floor with a scrutinization that made Idalia's toes curl.

"You would know what that looks like, wouldn't you, Calliope?" The Prince who had since been silent spoke harshly, which drew Idalia's attention back to him. The woman rolled her emerald eyes and the Prince that she accompanied interrupted her from speaking further.

"Are you a criminal?" The meaner of the two Princes quipped.

"A criminal with a conscience, that would be a new one." The woman, Calliope, cackled to herself as she took another drink.

Idalia swallowed, "Yes." She let her eyes settle on a patch of red veins in the black marble flooring.

"Oh, we never did clean that up after the last visitor." The first Prince tapped his chin and she suddenly realized that the discoloration of the marble was not naturally occurring. That was dried blood.

"State your crime." He leant forward on his throne.

Idalia paused. She needed to make it appear as if she was unwilling to admit what she had done. "Murder."

"Well, the population on your side of the Gate has been increasing, so you may have done all of us a favor." He chuckled, and she had never thought that a noise typically reserved for lighthearted situations could sound so ominous.

"However," he continued, "I am sure you're familiar with the law. A life for a life or torture for the same number of years as the number of deaths accrued." The Prince recited, almost as if the law excited him. Idalia suddenly got a heavy sinking feeling in the pit of her stomach.

"How many counts?" The second Prince questioned, and now the tally of how many times that he spoke so far rested at a mere two.

"One." Idalia shifted away from the stain on the ground.

"Then you will remain imprisoned here for a singular year, until your execution on this same date." The first Prince concluded, and he toyed with the chain around his neck. *He could strangle someone with that,* Idalia supposed.

"Erin, take her to the cells, and perhaps throw in a few fun activities to reward her bravery for crossing over."

Erin nodded and stepped off the ledge to haul Idalia to her feet. "You would have been better off just living with your guilt." He glanced at his brother and chuckled. *Both of them had such alarming laughs. The vocal embodiment of a ominous secret or an underlying threat.*

Erin's cool fingers latched onto her wrist, and he dragged her away into an adjacent corridor. With his grip of granite, she understood why they had not exchanged the ropes for shackles. "I'm not sure if you're alarmingly stupid or incredibly brilliant." Erin all but shoved her into a dark, windowless room.

"Is this to be my prison then?"

Idalia heard the unmistakable sound of an iron latch sliding into place, and then footfalls in the darkness. "What is it with you and jumping to conclusions?" Erin stood not two feet in front of her, but her eyes had yet to adjust.

"Excuse you, Prince, you know nothing about me." She folded her arms, "And it's not jumping to conclusions if you have common sense."

A laugh. A strangely melodic one this time.

"I know that you're a Sentry, have a penchant for holding on to your aces, and-" Idalia heard the uncanny echo of a match striking stone right before light filled the space. "Are quite skilled at making weapons out of discarded liquor bottles."

It couldn't be...

In the light of the lanterns and candlesticks, Idalia stared at Erin in both awe and bewilderment. She should have looked upon him in fear. After all, he was a Prince of the Gate. But to her, she could not differentiate between this

Prince and the young man that played cards with her after she tried to arrest him.

"Keir-" She breathed and then immediately brought her still-bound hands to her mouth. She probably shouldn't have said that.

"While that's probably not a name that we should use here, I won't throw you in the dungeon for recognizing my alter ego." Erin shook his head. His hair looked different, his... everything looked different.

"How is this possible? You're... not you-" Idalia tried to wrap her mind around it all, and then something else stole her focus. "Wait!" She gasped, "When I stopped you- I was right! I did trust my gut."

"I told you to trust your instincts, Idalia, you didn't catch a criminal that night, you caught the Prince of them." A smirk danced on his lips.

"Yes!" She laughed, and then drew in a breath. "Oh..." She adjusted her posture and held her shoulders back. This *wasn't* the boy who played cards with her. She needed to remember that.

"No need to be alarmed, Idalia. I've still got a card game to win." He chuckled, and the noise sounded much softer this time than it had before. Idalia found that she preferred this laugh much more. This one could chase the shadows away, rather than lure them in.

Her shoulders relaxed a touch, although every bone in her body told her to be on guard.

"Now that we've gotten the introductions out of the way, care to tell me why you're actually here?" Erin leaned against a large black dresser so casually that if she wasn't aware of his rank, she would have forgotten that a Prince stood a mere four feet in front of her.

"What do you mean? You heard why I got sent over." Idalia's eyes fell to the ground, feigning guilt. It appeared that the same onyx-colored marble flooring spread through the entire castle. Thankfully, she could not see any ruby stains interwoven in this space.

Erin surveyed her for a moment. She could barely hear him breathe in the quiet.

"How did you do it?" He responded thoughtfully.

Idalia shifted her wrists in the bindings uncomfortably. Trevor and Mox had told her to state her crime, but they had brushed over exactly how she committed it.

"Dagger to the chest." She replied.

When she snuck a glance at Erin, she saw nothing in his expression but to her surprise he came over and untied the ropes on her wrists. When she was free, she rubbed where the skin would surely bruise.

"You can sit at the vanity." He inclined his head in the direction of a dark gilded mirror and crimson velveteen stool that she had not noticed before.

Idalia lingered where she stood for a heartbeat before she moved toward his request. Erin came up to stand beside her, and they both looked at each other in the mirror for a mere moment.

Then he tore his gaze away and reached a hand up to curl a lock of her light-brown hair around his finger. A breath escaped Idalia as she watched her hair darken at the roots, bleeding down the tresses with the color of a raven's feather in the dead of night. "What are you doing?"

"For all anyone knows, you're wasting away in a cell right now. It would raise their suspicions if anyone saw you freely wandering the grounds." He spoke softly.

She knew it wasn't wise to ask, but her curiosity got the best of her. "Why? I mean, what do you gain from not throwing me in prison?"

Erin's hand hovered over Idalia's shoulder, "I told you; we have a card game to resolve." She caught the near imperceptible way that his lips tugged upwards.

He didn't look how the stories portrayed him. There was just enough dangerous beauty to his features to be alluring, but Idalia didn't find his face threatening. If anything, there was a certain softness to his caramel eyes that appeared when the candlelight struck them a specific way. "Is this how you treat all unwanted guests?"

Erin touched three fingers to her shoulder, and her complexion shifted. Erasing her tan and the freckles that came with it. "Only the ones that nearly slit my throat in alleyways."

Idalia watched her transformation in the mirror. She began to look unrecognizable even to herself. Her eyebrows were darkening, while her upper lip thinned, and her bottom lip became fuller in appearance. Even her nose straightened itself out, where it used to turn down at the tip.

Somehow, he gave her the illusion of wearing cosmetics with a flush to her newly pale cheeks and a deep red rouge to her lips. Even her lashes appeared to be painted black, like the women she would see strolling the streets of the upper end of Thulta.

"I didn't know you could do this; didn't all magic die out?" She murmured, trying to get accustomed to staring at a strange face in the mirror.

"It's a gift." He replied, "I can change my own appearance, and yours." Erin gestured to his face, "This is real, more or less."

"Which is it?" Idalia quipped, fidgeting with her hands in her lap.

"Pardon?" His fingers paused right over her pulse, and she could feel the cool metal of his rings as they pressed against her bare skin. *One adorned every finger.*

"More, or less?"

"Don't you think you've gotten enough information out of me for one day?" He raised a perfectly groomed, black eyebrow at her reflection.

Right. Information. The whole reason why they put her here in the first place. He made this unknowingly all too easy for her.

"Thank you." Idalia spoke, running a hand through her hair. Even the texture was different. She looked as if she'd been pampered and taken care of her entire life. Looks could be so misleading.

"This is one of my private quarters, you can have the space to yourself but keep the door locked. No one should bother you. If they do, tell them you know me." Erin dropped his hands back to his sides and stepped away from the vanity.

"Should I have a different name too?" Idalia crossed the room toward the ornate candlesticks.

Erin shook his head, causing his well-combed hair to fall in his face. "They don't know your name, and it'll be too risky for you to remember an alias." He spoke with such certainty that Idalia wondered if he was speaking from experience. Why would a villainous Prince of the Gate need a disguise?

She tipped her chin in understanding and watched as he walked to the door, but Erin paused before the threshold. "You know, you should have used a different lie earlier. If you had said the weapon you used was a bottle neck, I would have *almost* believed you." A glint caught in his caramel eyes as he glanced over his shoulder.

He knew she lied. Then why extend this kindness? Before she could formulate a response, he slipped out of the room, and she hurried to relock the door upon his exit. Idalia leant against the wall and loosed a breath. This felt too easy; she had never expected such an opportunity to just fall into her lap. She could get close to Erin, it seemed that she already had an in with him, for some reason.

She wasn't sure what twist of fate to thank, but as she lay amongst the black silk sheets of the lavish bed that night, only one thing circulated in her mind.

This could be possible.

Chapter Eight
Don't Look Too Deep

Over the course of the next six nights, Erin brought Idalia dinner and a deck of cards. They ate together, a Prince of the Gate and a Sentry. At the end of their visit Erin always paused the game, saying they would simply continue it tomorrow. Then tomorrow would come and he would utter the same words with a smile.

On the seventh night of her stay there, Erin arrived at the room earlier than usual. They had devised a secret knock that gave Idalia assurance to open the door. With such precautions being taken, one might think that they were young lovers sneaking around after midnight instead of two souls in the process of forming a friendship.

A friendship based on an act is no friendship at all. Idalia reminded herself.

"Tell me, would it go against your moral code to dine with a family of royal crooks?"

Idalia drummed her fingers on her arm. "Seeing as I have been dining with one member of that family for the past week, I'd say my moral code allows exceptions."

"Good, as tonight is the weekly banquet, and I find myself in need of a date." He bowed at the waist, and Idalia couldn't help but smirk at the absurdity of it all. *A Prince, bowing to her.*

"I fear if I refuse, these lovely accommodations will be stripped away." She flung her arm out at the room and the several gowns that Erin had brought to her which peppered her scarlet and onyx bedspread.

Erin extended his bent elbow, "You fear correctly, rejecting a Prince of the Gate has sore repercussions."

If his brother had been the one to utter those words, Idalia would have felt a knot tighten in her stomach. But Erin said them so easily, and near lightheartedly that she only felt amused.

"Wait." She tugged on his sleeve to get him to stop before he reopened the door. "What is my role tonight?"

Erin studied her for a moment, "Stay close by, don't give anyone anything to use against you. Above all, forgive me in advance for what I may say."

Idalia readjusted her hand placement on his arm. How bizarre. A Prince asking *her* for forgiveness.

As Erin led her from the room down the many twisting corridors and hallways, Idalia tried her best to make a mental map of the layout if there ever became a need to flee. There were an unholy number of doors down every path. She wondered if all of them housed criminals and thieves, or did each member of the royal family have their own wing in this massive place?

They came to a crossroads in the hall, and while Erin turned them to the right, Idalia couldn't help but steal a glance at what lay in the other direction. The only thing that she captured was the lack of torches littering the walls. The very wallpaper appeared to be coated in grease and had peeled from where it met the façade. The unkempt look of the hallway only added to the ominous feel.

Idalia wasn't sure what to expect as they reached the double doors. If she had to venture a guess of what she would see when they entered the dark dining hall, it would consist of a lavish ballroom filled with well-dressed thieves and villainous friends of the crown. As they entered, however, Idalia realized that her guess was quite wrong. The ebony dining table indeed appeared to be burnished with gold, but the only bodies in attendance were her and Erin, his brother, and the woman who had laughed at Idalia upon her judgement.

"Well, this is a new development, dear brother." Erin's brother twirled an unfortunately stained blade between his scarred fingers. "When were you going to tell us you acquired a damsel?"

Calliope scanned Idalia from head to toe and thank the Author that no recognition flickered in those soulless green eyes of hers.

Erin glanced over at Idalia briefly and took his seat. "I'm still unsure whether or not I'll tire of her shortly, Lester." He took an apple from the table and tossed it up in the air, catching it with ease. "I figured that she'd do for tonight." His lips pulled back into a cruel smirk.

His brother chuckled, clearly entertained by Idalia's presence, and gestured for a servant to pour the wine. The servant in question stood at a staggering height and boasted a horrific scar down the left side of his face.

"Do you have a name, Pet?" Lester's gaze settled on Idalia, and it felt suffocating. He possessed the sort of gaze that could stifle a soul or melt through iron if he willed it. She dined with the man who could very well be her executioner if she did not pull this off.

"Idalia, my Prince." *Oh, how she hated to even feign respect for this man.*

"Sorry hon, that would be *my* Prince." Calliope gave a laugh that made the hair on Idalia's arms stand up as the wicked woman curled her fingers onto Lester's collar.

"Careful, I'll get jealous." Erin coolly slid his gaze over to Idalia, and she wasn't sure what on earth possessed her to respond but she did.

"Why would you be jealous, weren't you tiring of me?" She quirked a brow.

A hushed silence fell over the table, and Idalia wondered if she had gone too far. Then Lester laughed and smacked the table, causing the delicate glassware to shake, and Idalia was quite certain that the silverware jumped. "Say, Erin, when she no longer suits your fancy send her my way."

Calliope looked as disgusted as Idalia felt. Something in her felt pity for the woman, so she spoke again, "Is she not your intended?"

If Lester felt any surprise at being spoken to so boldly, he did not show it. Or perhaps that was a distraction so that she would not expect it when he hurled that two-toned knife at her chest.

Lester waved a lazy hand, his pewter rings glinting in the candlelight. "Do you see a ring on her finger?" He followed his words with a dark laugh.

Calliope slowly uncurled her hand from his collar, and shifted in her seat, suddenly rendered silent. Indeed, when Idalia looked closely, there was no band there. *Still...*

"Now that we've established the dynamics at this table." Erin drawled, looking bored, "Can we eat?"

Lester snapped his fingers, and several servants lifted the black domes from their dishes. To her surprise, there were a multitude of options, but how? Everything here was so barren and decayed. Right as Idalia stabbed what appeared to be fish of some variety with the tines of her fork, she felt an unsettling tingling trail over her forearm. She glanced down and did a double take. There was writing forming on her skin, cursive to be exact. The jet-black ink appeared letter by letter. Idalia did not dare to look over at Erin, but he had to be the one doing this. The tingling sensation paused a second later, and she read what he had etched onto her skin.

Don't eat that.

She turned her arm over, keeping it hidden under the deep ruby table runner and gently shook the bite off her fork. In her periphery, she noted that Erin also did not touch the fish on his plate. *Strange.* The next time that Idalia peered at her arm, it was as bare and untouched as before, with no trace of any lingering letters. *Perhaps that was another way that Erin could manipulate her appearance.*

The rest of the meal was eaten in silence, save for a few scattered crude comments from Lester after his third glass of wine. Calliope's jaw was set in a firm line, and the dark dagger-like glares that Idalia was met with each time their eyes locked were not lost on her.

When Erin stood up from the table, Idalia took that as her cue to follow him. It wasn't until they were safely back in her room that she felt she could breathe. Erin tugged his collar loose and sighed. "You definitely made an impression tonight."

"I'm sorry, I should have held my tongue."

Erin chuckled warmly, "No, your comments were the most entertaining part of the night."

Some tension evaporated from her shoulders, "Tell me if I cross a line, with us."

Erin looked confused, "What do you mean?"

"I mean, I don't want to take advantage of your kind-ness." *That was a lie*, and she knew it. The whole purpose of this was to get close to him. "I know you rank higher."

Erin slung his arm over the side of the chaise as he plopped down. "When it comes to me, I want you to forget about this rank nonsense. To be quite honest with you, I would abdicate if I could."

Why did that not surprise her? "How are you so different from them? I've heard horror stories of the both of you."

Erin twirled a golden band on his thumb, "The major-ity of those stories are more than likely regarding Lester. Don't get me wrong, I've-" he paused, "I've had to do certain things that I don't agree with but sometimes..." He sighed and looked up at the ceiling to the dark crys-tal chandelier that hung there. "Sometimes you spend so long pretending to be something that you're not, and even then, you don't get the results you wish you had."

Idalia sunk into the opposing chaise. "Have you ever considered just running away?" She should dig while he's vulnerable. See what information she could retrieve, but right now? Idalia just wanted to learn more about him... *the real him.*

Erin tipped his head back and laughed, "Only every day of my life."

Something in Idalia came undone. While she had been striving her entire life to belong and cement her place in this world, Erin had so desperately desired to escape his place.

"Then why don't you?" She questioned quietly. "You could change how you look and start fresh."

Erin opened his mouth and then closed it, as if hesitant for what would come next. "I'm a part of something big here. I can't leave, not when we're so close to making a breakthrough."

Idalia stayed quiet. *Something big, like unleashing a war on Thulta?* She made a mental note to include that in her report tonight.

"Now that I've laid bare that secret." He chuckled,

"Might I ask one of you?"

Idalia snapped back to attention and nodded.

"That night at the Tap." He started, "You said that you named yourself?"

Oh, he remembered that?

"Yes, I-" Idalia dug her fingernails into her palm, indenting the skin in little half-crescents. "I don't know what name my parents had for me; I can't remember."

Something akin to sympathy lay heavy in his eyes.

"Were they killed?"

Idalia shifted on the chaise; She had liked the look of the burgundy damask gown when she had donned it earlier, but now the bodice was beginning to feel incredibly tight. "I don't know. I went to sleep in my childhood bed when I was five and woke up alone on the orphanage's porch."

Erin was quiet for a long minute; it sounded as if the world was holding its breath. Or maybe that was just her.

"I'm so sorry, Idalia."

She shrugged a shoulder, "I only remember pet names, so I guess I never paid attention to my real name."

"Hey, maybe you dodged a dagger. They could have named you something like, Myrtle." Erin offered, clearly trying to lighten her mood.

A small, half-smile pulled at her lips. "Maybe."

Erin pushed himself off the chaise, "I'll let you get some rest."

"What, no card game?" Idalia smiled more freely now at the change in topic.

A mischievous smirk toyed with his features, "Tomorrow." With that he slid the bolt back from her door and slipped out of the room.

Chapter Nine
His Watchful Gaze

There was stationery in one of the desk drawers. Idalia took a piece and brought it to the light of a lamp before she began to write. In the note, she added everything of significance that she could remember since she crossed the Gate. She mentioned that one Prince was a part of something big, but she could not bring herself to expose Erin as the royal in question. When she sealed the letter, she felt rotten. As if she had eaten something that turned her stomach sour.

Idalia waited until she heard complete silence before she left her room. She wandered around on silent feet. Every main door would be guarded, she was sure of it. But if she could find the kitchen...

It was more difficult to navigate this labyrinth in the dark but at least tonight's full moon shed enough light that she wouldn't trip over her own feet. Idalia took enough left turns to stumble across the kitchen. When she pushed open the door, she realized that the space was unnecessarily gigantic. *They could probably feed half of Thulta in here, or at least the part that she was from.*

Idalia located the exit door and carefully slid the latch into place. While the rest of the palace seemed grand and overtly ornate with its touches of gold and scarlet amongst the black, the chef's door was held up with crude bits of wood and rope splintering at the corners.

When Idalia stepped out, she inhaled deeply. She supposed that there was a benefit to a land so dark. The stars burned more brightly here than she'd ever seen in Thulta. She settled her hand over the letter tucked safely underneath her belt and started for the southwest side of the Gate.

In the west wing of this cold castle, a young man with peculiar caramel eyes watched from his window as a girl hurried to slip a scrap of paper underneath a moss covered stone.

And he smiled.

The Murmur

*S*omething unexpected occurred when I met her. One look into her eyes and I saw conviction laid bare. Honesty overflowing, and the radiance of a pure heart. Under all that, was such a desire to belong, that she lost sight of the fact that she was more worthy to lead than any one of us. So, if you ask me why I trusted her so completely, so quickly?

Because she embodied something I wished I could have again.

Light.

Chapter Ten

Take Me To Paradise, Won't You?

The days flew by, and one week turned into two, which morphed into four. Before Idalia knew it, she had managed to live in the heart of the Gate for a month and a half. She knew that it was dangerous for Trevor to keep up any correspondence on his end. Every time her letter would be gone and there would never be a new one in its place.

Erin would come by and talk to her every night, without fail. She found solace in his company, even if they just sat in peaceful quiet.

Tonight, Erin snuck a treat from the kitchen. Popped corn kernels with butter. Idalia found that she liked the taste very much.

"Your turn. Where would you go if you had the chance? Would you leave Thulta?" Erin tossed a piece of the corn into his mouth and looked at her.

Idalia propped herself up on her elbows and thought about it. "Somewhere with a waterfall."

"A waterfall, huh? Any particular reason?"

Idalia nodded her head emphatically, causing a ringlet to slip out of her hairpin. "There was a book at my orphanage. It told of this wondrous place with waterfalls, exotic birds, and the most breathtaking flowers. So many nights I wished I could simply leap into the pages and live there."

Erin seemed to ponder this for a minute, and then he dusted his hands off and stood to his feet, "Come on."

"Wha- it's your turn next."

He gave her a gentle smile, "And I will give you an answer, I promise." He offered his hand to her, clearly adamant in his resolve. She gave him a questioning look but slipped her hand into his and he helped her to her feet.

"Where are we going?" Idalia whispered when they were out in the hall.

"If I tell you, it negates the point of a surprise." Erin winked, and his eyes dazzled from the flickering light of the sconces.

Idalia squeezed his hand in jest as they took off down a corridor. It felt like they'd walked for hours, and all the halls started to bleed together. How could anyone keep track of them all?

He pushed open a couple of doors and suddenly she felt a change in the ground beneath her shoes. Soft, like grass. Erin stepped in front of her and took her by the shoulders. "Swear you won't say a word about this." He said seriously, and then an amused smirk pulled at his sensuous lips. "They'll kick me out."

Idalia nodded, curiosity filling her up to the very brim as he turned to open the final lattice door. *The door that led to paradise*. Idalia devoured the scene with wide eyes. Lush green grass formed the thickest blanket at their feet, while the aroma of a multitude of flowers wafted up to her nose. The atmosphere was completely enclosed by archways of curving trees. To her left, she could hear something strangely reminiscent of the sound of rushing water.

"How is this..."

"Possible?" Erin finished. "It was my mother's." He knelt down in front of Idalia and gently took her foot, slipping off one heel at a time and setting them aside so that she could feel the soft earth. "It was her secret oasis, and when she passed, it became mine."

Idalia was near breathless from the beauty of it all. She crouched to run her fingertips over a delicate purple and blue petal. "What happened to her?"

Erin turned a palm leaf over between his fingertips.

"She was killed in the uprising."

Idalia hesitated, "I'm so sorry."

Erin let the palm leaf brush his shoulder as he walked further into the greenery. "It's alright, I believe that she got her wings. Although, she was the type of person to give away all her feathers." Idalia settled her hand on his forearm when she heard his voice tighten. *He must have deeply loved her.*

"I didn't know there was an uprising here." She added after a moment of silence.

Erin made an acknowledging noise. "There was a time when the outcasts were not as afraid of my family. They banded together and attacked when we were weakest."

Idalia had never considered the fact that wars surely broke out amongst those within the Gate.

"Follow me, you haven't seen the real reason I brought you here." He rolled his shoulders as if shaking off the memory and took her hand, leading her up a set of stone steps.

"Look down." He waved a hand, and she couldn't help the smile that lit up her every feature.

"It's wonderful." She breathed. A small waterfall rushed and splashed over smooth round boulders, and the water itself sparkled as if made of magic.

"I want you to come here whenever you want, hopefully it'll make these cold walls feel less like a prison." Erin smiled softly at her.

"Thank you, although how about we come here together, I don't know where I'd end up if I tried to make the trek alone."

Erin stayed quiet. Then she realized he wasn't looking at the stunning scenery. His gaze was stuck on her. "Go ahead, explore." He said after a moment.

Idalia lingered, as if she wanted to speak again but the words simply would not come. So, she slipped off into the lush foliage to be closer to the waterfall.

Erin eased himself to the ground, watching her smile as water from the stream splashed over her fingertips.

The Murmur

*B*y the Author, she was imperfect. In the same way that a snowflake is imperfect. Graceful and dainty and lovely, but sharp and jagged and oh so complicated when one looks closer.

I wanted to look closer.

Chapter Eleven
A Ball, a Hall, Their Downfall

This family truly was like the nobility of old. Except, only villainous. Idalia could hear the clanking of champagne flutes and roaring laughter all the way from her quarters as she worked to get a wrinkle out of her skirt. Erin had warned her about the semi-annual balls that were held, and naturally about all the less than savory types that frequented these cold halls for the night. Four raps of knuckles on wood filled Idalia's ears and she abandoned pressing the hem of her gown. She slipped the chain away from the lock and cracked the door open for him.

"I'm sorry, am I interrupting you?" Erin hung his head, and one hand shielded his eyes from potentially invading her privacy.

"No, you're just fine. I'm ready, all that's left is for me to fix this necklace." She waved him in.

"Oh good." Erin slumped into his favorite chaise and rubbed at his temples.

"Are you okay?" Idalia questioned as she shifted the chain of the knotted necklace from hand to hand.

A pause. Then, "Lester is having one of his days." He exhaled sharply through his nose and then finally looked at her, "Oh, you look lovely."

Idalia fought a blush, "You're just trying to butter me up, so I go easy on you with our cards tonight."

Erin shook his head but didn't say anything further on the topic. Idalia laid the chain down on the dark table and retrieved a small pin from the drawer. "What's Lester doing to cause that headache of yours?"

"How did you know I have a-" Erin cut himself off when Idalia mirrored his previous gesture of massaging his temples. "It's nothing for you to worry about, just act normal. I fear any change will set him off further."

Idalia paused prodding the tangle in the necklace and studied Erin for a second. "If I know what's wrong, it will better prepare me for tonight."

Erin interlocked his fingers and stretched them over his head, closing his eyes as the motion relaxed his tired muscles. "Dahlia haven't you ever heard the phrase, "Curiosity killed the cat?"

She opened her mouth to interject but then stopped.

"You'd think after a month and a half of living here you'd know my name."

He slit one eye open to look at her and then closed it. "I know it."

She playfully pointed the silver pin in his direction, as if it was a sword she would use to duel with.

"Perhaps you have me confused with another lady friend."

That made him open both eyes. "No, your name has a flower in it, and I find that sweet."

He probably got that love of horticulture from his mother.

"Fine, I'll let you off easy. Once." Idalia turned back to her necklace.

"Do you want me to try?" He asked, rolling onto his side and propping his head up with his elbow.

She shrugged one shoulder, "Sure."

Erin left his spot on the chaise to join her and bent over the dainty chain. "I should have known not to trust a Sentry with such delicate jewelry." A glint of amusement shimmered in his eyes.

"For your information, I was quite gentle with it. Until I accidentally dropped it behind the dresser." Idalia confessed and placed the pin on the table beside his hand.

Erin chuckled and eased the knot from the metal. "You're so unpredictable." He mused, dropping a tangle-free necklace into her open palm.

"It's a gift." Idalia flashed a grin and secured the chain around her neck.

Erin only gave her a small smile in return and turned on his heel for the door. Tired, she thought. *He looked so tired.*

"Hey, are you sure you want to make an appearance tonight?" She softened her tone.

Erin rolled his shoulders, "Someone's got to keep these felons in line." He offered a more at-ease smile this time, and it was enough to settle that tiny bit of concern that waved in her head.

"Then I will happily accept your princely escort, milord." Idalia dropped into a small, lighthearted curtsy.

She had intended for the gesture to make him laugh or at least crack a smile. She would have even taken the slightest way that his eyes crinkled when he was trying not to laugh. But Erin only offered her his suited arm, and he turned his face from her.

The rest of the evening went as Idalia expected, although she was not a fan of the not-so-subtle way that Lester watched her from his throne. She had the uncanny feeling that she was becoming a different type of prey entirely.

Erin had been acting... off, for the past several hours and Idalia was determined to figure out why. However, if he confided in her, she would omit what he said from her letter tonight.

"Wanna continue our game?" Idalia fumbled with the door handle, as her silk glove made the metal too slippery to latch onto. Eventually, she pulled the fabric off with her teeth and slipped inside, waiting for Erin to follow.

"Not tonight. I'm sorry. I-" Erin massaged a pressure point at the back of his neck. "Tomorrow?" He questioned, and Idalia caught a tone of sheepishness in his voice.

"That's fine. Erin, are you sure you're okay?"

He leant his shoulder against the door casing and twirled a pewter ring on his index finger. "Careful Jewel, you're sounding attached." He replied with an easy smile.

Another nickname, that was twice in one day.

"So do I take that as a yes or...?" Idalia tilted her head, and her black waves slid behind her shoulder, leaving it bare.

Erin dipped his chin once, "Get some rest, I'll see you tomorrow."

Idalia had always been one for rules. A few months ago, she would have thought twice about breaking etiquette, royal or otherwise. But Erin had become her friend, it was as if everything that defined him as a villainous Prince merely followed him like a shadow that he couldn't escape.

So, Idalia said goodnight, and several moments after he left, she crept back out behind him. Her mind twirled with various notions of what could be causing this drain on Erin. Lester naturally came to mind first. Just being in that man's general vicinity gave her the impression that he was akin to a leech, sucking whatever dignity and pride a person held until they were just a husk of their former self.

It could also be the stress from running half a kingdom of criminals and killers. If that was a factor, then how could she help? Before her stay across the Gate, the closest she had ever been to royalty was when King Damien's eldest son and his wife visited her orphanage, looking for a trophy-child to display. Although she was not chosen, she felt no jealousy for the one that was. When she saw him years later, they had groomed him and changed him into someone nearly unrecognizable. In that moment, Idalia knew that the same boy who helped her dig up earthworms would not be caught dead with dirt on his crisp white linen shirt.

Idalia had gotten so caught up in reminiscing that she almost missed a flicker of movement heading into the adjacent corridor. The strange one with oily wallpaper and virtually no light.

She peeked around the corner, holding her breath so that she wouldn't be exposed. After all, what could she say to explain herself if this shadowy silhouette was not Erin?

Better question, what would she say if it was?

Then a door opened, and the light inside spilled out into the hallway, offering a faint glow to everything and everyone in it. When Idalia's eyes adjusted, she clenched her fist so hard that her nails dug into her palm and bent. Erin walked through a door that someone held ajar.

And that someone was Calliope.

Chapter Twelve
Can You Lie To Me?

Idalia had more questions than answers, and she wasn't quite sure how to handle them. She just couldn't picture Erin and Calliope sneaking around together and the image that her mind presented made her stomach turn. Surely, that was not the case. Idalia stopped herself when she re-entered her room and locked the door. What was it to her even if it was? He was a free man, a Prince. It wasn't as if she would lose his friendship over this new development. She rolled her shoulders and sat down to quickly write her report.

As Idalia wrote, her mind wandered. What sort of plans were Trevor and the others building with the information that she gleaned? She had yet to hear anything about an impending war. The closer she got to Erin, the worse it made her feel that she could have a hand in the downfall of his family. Lester, she wouldn't mind knocking down a few pegs. But Erin?

This was your chance to prove yourself, remember?

Idalia shook her cloak from its haphazard sprawl on the marble and put it on. As she headed toward the kitchen, she couldn't help but spare a passing glance down that dark hallway. She could see a soft, budding light peek out from underneath the door, and long shadows moved fluidly along the floor. Idalia closed her fist around the envelope as a tinge of loneliness spread through her in a wave. She wasn't unfamiliar with the sensation, but she had yet to feel that way with Erin. Perhaps this was a good reminder that she couldn't get too attached. Idalia should not expect him to divulge every secret to her when she was clearly not willing to do the same.

She knew this.

So why did it sting?

The dead grass crunched and crumpled underneath her shoes as she straightened. Another letter lay pressed into the dirt, hidden by that mossy rock. If only the Princes knew what she was. Divulging every detail of anything they let slip to their enemies. She'd be killed on the spot.

For some reason, the odds that she had survived this long nearly made her laugh. She was playing a strange game of luck and chance, but the problem was that all games end eventually. There could come a point where there would not be a tomorrow to resume it.

Just as she pivoted on her heel to leave, she heard rustling from behind her and she froze in her tracks. She could hear breathing, but it sounded as if this intruder was just as afraid of being caught as she was. Idalia glanced back and relief enveloped her as she moved closer to the Gate.

"Trevor." *He had come. It was so good to see a familiar face.*

Trevor balked, "How do you... how do you know my name?" His voice was cautious, guarded.

"What?" Idalia blinked. Then she realized when she looked at the hands that clasped the bars of the Gate, that her pale complexion would be as foreign to him as it once was to her.

"It's me." She whispered. *She was treading on dangerous waters right now.*

"Dilly?" He squinted in the dark, "Is this a trick?"

She shook her head, and a laugh threatened to bubble up in her throat, "No, it's just to fit in. What are you doing here?"

The moon slid out from the canopy of clouds that blocked its light, and Trevor could finally see her fully. His eyes tracked over her, although some details were lost to the shadows of night. "You look... really good, different but-" he tilted his head, which made him look more boyish than she'd remembered, "good."

Idalia uncurled her fingers from the bars to smooth down the folds in her cloak. If she had known she would be under such careful scrutiny, perhaps she would have run a brush through her hair. "Thank you." She murmured.

"You still didn't tell me why-" Idalia started, but he interjected.

"My conscious got the better of me." Trevor admitted, and Idalia could have sworn that she heard an edge of worry creep into his voice. "We shouldn't have sent you here all alone." His voice dropped to a whisper, and the gentle breeze carried it to her ears.

"I heard you, you know. You all thought I was expendable."

Trevor sucked in a slight breath, "I don't feel that way."

Idalia studied him, "You're actually here to check on me?"

He nodded, "I realized that we sent you into the deep end with practically no way to protect yourself."

If she had no way to protect herself, she wouldn't still be standing in front of him. "A little warning would have been nice, but this is my job, isn't it?"

Trevor's shoulders slumped at her words. "Dilly..."

Idalia had forgotten how much she hated that name. She shook her head and backed up a step. One. Two. Her back hit something behind her, and her heart leapt into her throat before she could draw in a breath. A heavy arm settled at her hip, keeping her close. Without looking, she knew who that limb and ornately decorated suit sleeve it wore belonged to.

"Is this boy bothering you, my love?"

Chapter Thirteen

Caught in More Ways Than One

E rin's voice was fierce enough to make the shadows scatter. Idalia's lips parted and closed, trying to form words but nothing came out in her cautious bewilderment. Erin twirled the tasseled rope of her cloak around his finger.

"You're awfully close to my domain." His eyes watched Trevor calculatingly. "Actually, you're touching something of mine." Erin lightly jerked his chin towards the Gate, that Trevor was still clutching with a white-knuckled grip. "If you leave now, I'll forget that you were looking at something of mine too." Idalia felt his fingertips graze her side through the cloak in one slow stroke, it didn't feel very *friendly* but Erin never broke eye-contact with Trevor long enough to notice the hitch in her breathing.

Trevor spared Idalia one last look, as if 'I'm sorry' could be conveyed in those two blinks, before he ran off to safety.

"Come on." Was all Erin said as he dropped his arm from her waist and clasped his hands behind his back as he walked into the palace.

Idalia had a horrible twisting sensation in her stomach as she fell into step beside him, *how could she explain this?* His silence was worse than any accusation or painful reprimand.

He opened the door to her quarters and ushered her inside, closing it behind them with a click. Erin leant back against a wall with his arms casually folded as if he hadn't just caught her conversing with one of the Gate's enemies.

"Say something?" Idalia muttered quietly. She braced for the disappointment, the betrayed look in his eyes.

Erin made a small noise in the back of his throat, "You're lucky it wasn't Lester or a guard that heard you tonight."

Idalia's head spun, "Excuse me?"

Erin tapped his fingers on his chest, "Maybe it's because I grew up in a den of thieves, but I was sneaking around better than that at 6 years old." A hint of a smirk danced on his lips.

"I'm confused." Idalia wrapped her arms around herself. If only she could wrap her mind around this the same way.

"I'm not." He walked over to her and gently unhooked the clasp of her cloak, pulling it from her shoulders before he laid it over a quilted chair the color of fine wine. Then he reached into his jacket pocket and withdrew a small object. An envelope, with a light coat of dirt on its surface. Idalia's gaze tracked from one of her letters, and back to him. "How long have you known?" She asked.

He eased down onto the chaise and beckoned her to sit as well. Idalia wasn't sure what to expect, but she listened.

"Over a month." He said simply. "I don't agree with him, you know. About you being defenseless." Erin spoke more softly into the silence.

He knew, and he had also heard everything that Trevor said to her.

"I'm not sure I understand." A part of her was scared to look at him in fear of what she would see in his eyes. *Or what she wouldn't see.*

"You're one of the good ones, Idalia. I knew it the night we met." He draped his arm over the chaise. "It only confirmed it when you came here, talking about this fictitious character that you killed with a dagger." A small laugh poured from his lips.

Idalia held her breath, "How did you know I made him up?"

Erin studied her for a long moment, "When you spend as much time as I have amongst killers, and… have been one yourself," he hesitated, "you learn pretty quickly how to separate the angels from the devils."

Idalia wanted to reach her hand out and comfort him, but she hesitated.

Erin continued, "Besides, watching you scramble away from the blood on the floor like it was infectious was a pretty good clue." He gave her a teasing grin.

"Why didn't you call me out on everything?"

Erin shrugged the shoulder that wasn't pressed against the face of the chaise. "Maybe I wanted to see how far you would go to keep this up. Or maybe I wanted you to want to tell me yourself."

Idalia gathered her knees up to her chest and rested her chin on them, "I get it, if you stop trusting me."

Erin tilted his head and reached out his hand to brush the side of her fingers with his own. "Are you up for a walk?"

Erin brought Idalia to his own room and left her to her own devices while he disappeared into what she could only assume was the adjacent washroom. This opulent space appeared to hold the same motif as the rest of the palace. Or so she thought, until she looked closer and could point out several touches that were reminiscent of him. A stack of worn leather journals on a table, two jackets carelessly slung over the bedpost, and framed pictures that appeared to be painted with gold leaf and onyx ink.

"I put away all the glass bottles, so I should survive," A warm voice reached Idalia's ears, and she turned to see him beside her. He kept his steps as quiet as softly falling snow. However, she was not looking at *him*, exactly.

"I don't know, I could still whack you over the head with that journal there." She jerked a thumb in the direction of his desk, and he smiled.

"Think you can spare an evening for your old friend, Keir?" He winked.

Idalia seemed to consider it, "You'll have to take it up with this Prince I know, he owes me two card games and may get jealous."

"I'm only the jealous type with one thing in my life," his gaze searched hers for a brief moment, "and apparently I owe her two games of cards."

Idalia fell silent, and Erin only smiled. *Would he be jealous of losing her friendship in the same way that she was worried about losing his to Calliope?*

A cheeky smile tugged on his lips again, "Don't tell me I've rendered you speechless."

Idalia gave him a light look and found that changing the subject was much easier than determining why exactly the English language was failing her.

"Do I need to look different again?" She questioned. If Erin had changed his appearance so that he would go unnoticed, wasn't she in danger of being seen by someone here if they were caught leaving?

Erin tugged his hand through his now-shorter hair, "Just try to stay as close to me as you can when we leave, I-" He studied her for a moment and then glanced down at his palm that he flexed. "Well to be honest with you my magic is stretched a little thin tonight."

Idalia tilted her head. *Honesty.* Why was he giving her even a sliver of that gift when she had not offered him much of it in return?

Maybe she should change that.

"You know if you're tired you can always take me on this 'walk' tomorrow."

Erin smiled again and Idalia noted that in this form, he had a dimple. "No, Jewel. it's important that you understand something tonight."

"You're in a cryptic mood." She mused.

"My livelihood is shrouded in mysteries, it's a hard habit to break." Erin chuckled and offered her his hand.

Idalia looked at his palm, the tone of his skin was much darker than his natural coloring, and the texture of it was different too. Rougher, like he spent his days working with them to craft something beautiful.

He did seem like the type of person to sculpt magic from thin air.

"I promise my tiredness is not contagious." Erin's voice held something distinctly teasing and Idalia realized that his hand was still outstretched and hovering in place, awaiting her own.

To correct her mistake, she took his hand. A tiny jolt of surprise went through her when he delicately interlocked their fingers instead of just covering her hand with his larger one.

"The kitchen isn't the only way out of here." His eyes lit with child-like mischief, as he quietly led the both of them away from the palace. The south portion of the Gate had bent bars, and if one was slim enough, they could slip right through with ease. Just like that, they left with nothing but the starlight and Erin's intuition to guide them.

There was something so daunting and reckless about it all, but also exciting. It was unheard of to leave the Gate, yet here she was. Escaping on a whim with one of its' Princes. The smiles that he tossed over his shoulder as they hurried a safe distance from the Gate made her stomach tumble with exhilaration. When they had officially entered Thulta, he threw back his hood and laughed.

"That worked a lot better than I imagined."

Idalia huffed, "I thought you had the utmost confidence that it would."

Erin gave her a sly grin, "What, do you think I'm always sneaking girls in and out of there?"

Idalia rolled her eyes and took a deep breath. The air had a distinct scent here, an amalgamation of hibiscus and the ocean. Across the Gate, things smelled burnt and stale. She never realized how she missed it. After all, Thulta was the closest thing that she ever had to a home.

"Now for the real reason I brought you over." Erin led her through two alleyways which were barely lit. He knew the route so well that she wondered if Erin could find this mystery destination with a blindfold.

Not more than seven minutes later did they arrive. A large rectangular building made of gray stone with a brown-brick roof stood in front of them. Despite it being night, Idalia could hear muffled conversations and laughter.

"What is this?"

"My honesty." He murmured and rapped on the door with his knuckles.

The wooden door swung open on its hinges to reveal a tanned woman with thick silver hair, probably in her late fifties. Idalia cocked her head; she could have sworn that the woman looked familiar. She had deep lines in her forehead, as if years of worry and aggravation had ingrained themselves on her skin. But, when she saw Erin, her features transformed into sheer happiness.

"Keir, sweetheart, what are you doing here?" She clasped her hands and then quickly ushered them in.

"Just checking in Mama Rose, I haven't been able to get away often enough." He settled a gentle hand on the shorter woman's shoulder.

"That is very correct, what has it been, three months?"

"Something like that." He slid her an easy grin, and then Mama Rose's eyes flicked to Idalia.

"Where in the stars are my manners, who is this little lady?" She beamed, and the beads that were interwoven into her hair made a playful melody.

Idalia had become accustomed to Trevor speaking on her behalf when someone asked after her name, and when Erin just waited patiently for her to answer herself, it took a second to register.

"Idalia, ma'am." She did a small polite curtsy of sorts, and Mama Rose cackled.

"Oh, sweet child save your bows, I'm not good enough for those." She elbowed Erin in the shoulder and Idalia saw a flicker of a secret joke pass between them.

"Prepare yourself, once I open this door, you'll be swarmed." Mama Rose warned. Idalia subconsciously inched closer to Erin's side, and she was unaware that she had moved at all until Erin rested his arm lightly around her shoulders in a comforting way.

The second door clicked open, and Idalia's jaw dropped at the number of residents in the room. There had to be a hundred of them, men and women alike. "Angel boy's back!" A little girl squealed, and Erin was promptly shoved to the hardwood by a stampede of little ones with no remorse.

"You kids are going to break my ribs if you get any bigger." He ruffled the hair of a boy that knelt next to them.

Idalia tried to stifle her laughter, but her efforts did not work all that well. Then, she felt a yanking tug on her skirt.

"You have really dark hair." A girl of around eight looked up at Idalia with curiosity turning her bright blue eyes into wide saucers. Erin leant back on his elbows as he listened intently to the varying and quite noisy stories that he was being told from the children.

"I'll let you in on a secret." Idalia whispered and then bent down to her height. "It's a magic trick." Idalia winked and the girl giggled.

"Come on little monsters, we're getting summoned." Erin got himself back to his feet with some effort, and even then, two smaller children hung onto his legs for dear life.

Idalia glanced back up and saw what he was talking about. Mama Rose had cleared two spots for them on the long benches in the room amongst the other adults. Erin stretched his legs out in front of him and Idalia perched on the edge, half-sitting on the cloak that she wore.

"So, what are you in for, pretty-thing." A different woman with short, choppy hair chittered from beside Idalia.

"In for? What do you mean?"

The woman slid a look to Erin, but he wasn't paying attention. "What's your story? everyone here has one."

Idalia shrugged one shoulder and the woman continued, "You're from the Gate, right? You have the look."

Idalia was about to answer when Mama Rose nudged a smooth wooden cup with a fragrant tea that smelled of jasmine into her hands. "Ellie don't overwhelm her. You remember how you were when you came here." Mama lightly reprimanded.

Ellie chuckled, "But if we get over the formalities now, then it won't be awkward. She's gonna have to talk if she's living here."

Erin cleared his throat pointedly and leant forward closer to them. "Els, I'm keeping this one with me."

Ellie seemed to think this over for a moment, and then a sly smirk tugged at her lips. "Oh, I get it. She's your Princess."

Idalia choked on the tea that she had taken a sip of, and Erin gently patted her back to coax the air to return into her lungs.

"Should I be offended at that reaction, Jewel?" He teased Idalia quietly and then said more loudly, "I wanted her to see what I'm proudest of."

Ellie seemed satisfied with that answer. When Idalia composed herself, she whispered to Erin, "She knows? About you being-"

"Royalty?" His smile made that dimple appear in his changed face.

"We all do." Mama Rose sat down with her own cup in front of them. "And it's a secret that every single one of us will take to our graves." She leant forward and patted Erin's knee much like a mother would. *Maybe that's why they call her mama.*

"What is this place?" Idalia questioned.

"Do you remember, when I told you that I was a part of something big?" Erin started, and then waved a hand towards those in the room. "All of these people, they had the death penalty on their heads."

Idalia held her breath, "But how are they all here?"

Erin rotated his cup in his hands, and his rings clinked against the wood. "My mother started this when she was our age. It's a reformation program. The Gate has an influx of criminals every day, and while Lester believes that they are killed or die from cruel torture, I move them. I try to work with them."

Idalia felt knots unravel in her mind, like a ball of string that started rolling to pave the way for her understanding.

That's what he had meant.

And she had told Trevor.

"Take me for example little love," Mama Rose tapped her cheek, where a long scar trailed from her cheekbone to the underside of her throat, "been here the longest, and probably deserved the worst."

Idalia looked at the woman, truly looked at her, and then things clicked into place. Years ago, she remembered seeing Mama Rose on wanted posters that were pasted around Thulta. She had run an illegal smuggling ring and was notorious for destroying those that got too hot on her trail. She hadn't been Mama Rose at that time, but 'Prickly Rose.'

"This boy's mama, grabbed on to whatever shred of light I had left and pulled me out of that dark place." She nodded thoughtfully, and Idalia couldn't believe that the woman sitting before her with a cup of tea and sparkly beads in her hair had ever been so cruel in her past life.

"And you've gone on to adopt all of these people as your own." Erin replied softly, a warmth in his voice that Idalia had noticed the last time that he brought up his mother.

"I always thought I had missed out when I was never able to have kids, but now I have too many to handle." She tipped her head back and laughed.

"That's... incredible." Idalia took Mama Rose's hand and gave it a gentle squeeze, which earned her a motherly smile in return. When she looked around at the faces in the room, nearly every one of them had been on their radar as Sentries. Some of them, she had a hand in sending through the Gate along with Trevor, Mox and Ben. Before, she had only thought that there were two sides to be a part of, but now she saw that there was another option. Idalia had the near-overwhelming sensation that she had spent her life on the wrong side.

"That's why you saved me too." She glanced into Erin's eyes.

Erin looked at her as if he was reading something that had been painstakingly written on her features, "That wasn't the only reason, Jewel, but I think I've given you enough of an information overload for one night." His strong hand rested on her forearm so lightly that she barely registered it.

"There's none finer than this one." Mama Rose shook her finger in Erin's direction. "Gets that patience of his from Sylvie."

Erin murmured something softly to Mama Rose and Idalia saw tears brimming in his caramel eyes. Sylvie must have been his mother's name. *This was what he fought for; this is what he was risking his life for. To give other people a second chance when everyone else said it wasn't worth the time.*

The little eight-year-old girl came back and sat next to Erin, leaning heavily on his shoulder like he was a giant teddy bear for her to snuggle with. "Did you marry Angel-boy?" She asked Idalia.

Erin cleared his throat, "You and your questions, Chelsea."

A nervous laugh slipped past Idalia's lips, "No, we're not... married."

"Why? He's sweet." She giggled and sprawled over his leg while still looking at Idalia.

"Why do you call him Angel-boy?" Idalia quipped, hoping for a change in topic because if this child kept on, Idalia feared that she would be at a loss for words.

"Cause he grants dreams. He found my daddy and the bad men stopped looking for us."

"The bad men?"

Chelsea sat up some and puffed her chest out, clearly trying to do an impression. "They all look the same."

Sentries. They had hunted down this little one's father.

"He's really good at it, ask him for something." She giggled, and Erin turned to Idalia with an amused look.

"I have to say, I'm quite curious what you'll pick myself."

Mama Rose came back around and scooped Chelsea up from Erin's lap. "It's past time for you to go to bed, your daddy nodded off two hours ago."

Chelsea pouted, "But I never get to see Angel-boy. Next time will take years." She whined.

"I'll come see you as soon as I can, promise." Erin gave her a soft smile, and Chelsea seemed to be weighing her options before she conceded with a little huff.

"This is really something special, Er-" Idalia caught herself, "Keir."

He rubbed the back of his neck and leant forward to rest his elbows on his knees. "I don't think there's anything greater that I could trust you with, if that answers your question from before."

Idalia mirrored his posture and twisted the chain around her neck absentmindedly.

"Thank you." She said in a quiet voice.

Erin only smiled.

Chapter Fourteen
Tell Me Your Wish

They spent another hour in the large home, sharing conversations and passing stories around with those adults who refused to sleep. Then Erin noticed the way Idalia's answers were becoming more mumbled, so he decided it was time for them to take their leave.

"Oh-" He muttered as they left, stopping Idalia in her tracks as he deftly tugged her hood back on over her hair. A lock of it curled around his index finger and he paused momentarily, just staring at it before he uncurled it and readjusted his own hood.

While sneaking out of the Gate was relatively simple, sneaking back in would be harder. They had to adjust their entry to the guards' rotation which Erin thankfully had memorized. When they were back in the palace, Erin opened her door before undoing his cloak and tossing it to the side. "So, what was it?" He questioned.

"Hmm?" Idalia unhooked her golden clasp.

"If you could have anything at all, what would it be?"

She stretched out on her bed and rolled over onto her stomach. "Unfortunately, I don't think it's anything you can give."

Erin watched her quizzically, "Humor me."

"A proper goodbye." She concluded, and the certainty with which the words left her mouth gave him the distinct impression that she had thought this through many times before.

"What do you mean?"

Idalia took a deep inhale through her nose and sat up. "I remember very little about my parents. I'm sure they had to give me up for a reason but-" Her fingernails dug harshly into the beaded comforter, the sensation a welcome distraction from the hurtful places that her mind tried to wander to.

"You wish they had told you goodbye?" There was something akin to an ache in his voice. Sympathy for her, as if his own bleeding heart could reach out and console the one that had shattered so many times.

"I never wanted much." She pulled her knees to her chest and hugged them. "Just for someone to love me and if they had to leave at least... tell me why." Idalia spoke that inner secret into the silence of the room.

"I bet your parents were wonderful at heart. They had to be to have you." Idalia didn't know when he moved but he now perched on the edge of the bed with his palm laid flat in front of her to take if she wished.

She did.

"You really think you've got me all figured out huh?" She gave a half laugh, but it lacked any humor.

"Only the important things, Jewel." Erin rubbed his thumb carefully over her soft hand.

"Besides, you can't ever have someone completely figured out. That's what makes knowing them interesting."

Idalia looked over their intertwined hands. "Why did you decide I was somebody to figure out? You could have brought me to that home after I came here."

Erin took a moment to ponder his wording. "If I had done that, I would be ridding myself of the company of an amazing woman."

Idalia lightly scoffed and picked at a thread in her dress with her free hand. "Erin, I just don't get it. I got sent here to spy on you, and yet you're trusting me so completely."

He looked at her, and Idalia felt the world's internal clock stop ticking. "I can't give you that goodbye that you want. What I can give you is my trust. And-" He gathered both of her hands in his own, "To trust me that I *won't* say goodbye."

There was such sincerity in his voice, that it practically bled through every word that he spoke. Idalia wanted to believe it, *Oh Author*, couldn't she believe it?

She could, because she realized in that moment, a heart will only break as long as you let it. Perhaps it was time to ask for help in bandaging those invisible wounds.

"I trust you."

Chapter Fifteen

Poisoned Dreams

A couple hours after Erin had left, Idalia heard a knock at the door and then the sound of scurrying footsteps. She cracked the door open and noticed a shining pewter tray holding a mug that rested next to the baseboard attached to her door. There was a small slip of paper that balanced on the top of the metallic cup and when she gathered the tray, she smiled.

Thought you'd enjoy this,

Erin

Idalia lightly kicked the door shut behind her with the back of her heel so that the scrumptious chocolate liquid would not splash to the floor. She curled up on the chaise and the heat from the mug thawed the chill in her hands. *How did he know how much she loved warmed chocolate?*

A contented sigh left Idalia's lips and she consumed half of the contents in the mug. The warmth seeped into her very mind, making her limbs heavy with exhaustion.

Before she knew it, night had stolen her away and she used its silence like a blanket.

In her dreams, her legs felt as heavy as lead and iron. She ran from something, past pillars of marble and stone. From someone, who called her name and begged her to stop but she didn't know where exactly it was that she was running to, just that she had to get there.

She stumbled across vines bearing the most jagged thorns which latched onto her skin, and when she tried to pry herself away she only tumbled into a deep, dark void.

Then she heard Erin's voice, "What have you done." He rasped, and when she pushed herself from the invisible ground her heart constricted. He was doubled over in agonizing pain, and a shadowed figure stood behind him, slowly sucking the last breaths from his lungs.

"No! Stop!" Idalia couldn't move. She couldn't crawl. She could only scream.

Strangled gasps left Erin's mouth as the figure stepped closer to them, and she saw blood trickle from his mouth.

"Get away from him!" She tore at the invisible bonds around her feet and wrists, but to no avail.

"Don't you know actions have consequences?" The figure spoke, and when it did, she felt everything crumple within her. Idalia knew that voice.

She heard it every time she opened her mouth.

The little bit of light that the nightmare offered her illuminated the very features that she used to see in the mirror. "I wouldn't do this to him-"

The wrong version of Idalia tapped her chin with the point of the dagger that she held.

"Isn't this what you've already done?" She questioned, and then abruptly froze and screeched, "Idalia!" over, and over until the very name became a murmured echo that lay trapped in her mind.

But it wasn't just in her head, the voice was morphing into one that sounded distinctly male. Though it was muffled, the better part of her subconscious felt a pull to the owner of the voice.

Help. She thought.

Chapter Sixteen
Promise That You'll Watch For Me

Idalia did not answer when Erin knocked the next day. It was approaching the evening, but he knew that she would never retire this early. He tried again, and when he heard no response, he let his hand settle on the doorknob. He could apologize for barging in on her privacy later, but something about this felt very unlike her. "Don't be locked, don't be locked." He muttered to himself, and thankfully the door pushed open with no interference.

"Oh no." Erin whispered a silent prayer when his eyes landed on her limp form, which was nearly falling off the chaise. There was little to no color left in her complexion and when he rushed to her side, her skin was uncomfortably hot to the touch.

"Idalia, what happened?" He gathered her up into his arms and laid her down on the bed before he searched for the root cause. Next to the chaise was a cup that had obviously been knocked over, staining a notecard with hastily scribbled writing on it. Erin kneeled to pick it up and fury ignited in his stomach as he let the now crumpled card drop to the floor unceremoniously. *He didn't send her this.*

Whoever did, clearly lacked the intelligence to understand that tampering with a Prince's Jewel struck a chord.

"Idalia, wake up for me." He turned his attention fully to the motionless girl atop the comforter. "Idalia?" He brushed the damp waves from her forehead. *Get the fever down, yes.*

As he stuffed cloths underneath the cool water, he racked his brain to recall anything about sickness and poisoning that he could. His father had been attacked on several occasions, but he had been too young to remember anything helpful. All that he recalled was the gentle murmur of his mother's voice as she cared for him. Despite everything that the King had put her through, she refused to let death sink its claws into him. Hopefully, his basic knowledge would be enough.

"While it's sweet that you trusted a notecard with my name on it, don't do that next time Dahlia." Erin cradled her head to slide one cool cloth underneath her burning skin.

"Stop-" She groaned, and his hand froze just above her forehead. He thought that perhaps he had her resting at a painful angle but then she muttered several things that had seemingly no correlation. It was then that Erin realized she was talking out of her head.

"You better fight this, we need to finish this game of ours." He smiled, but he knew that she wouldn't know. She probably didn't even hear anything that he said. But that was okay, perhaps it was to reassure himself, because something about sitting in silence with her in the room broke his heart.

"It's..." She nearly whispered, "Me."

Erin took her small hand in his own and was about to respond with something cheeky to fill the quiet but then she said hoarsely, "I'm sorry."

He saw tears bead underneath her lashes, and her eyebrows scrunched in pain.

By the Author, he just wanted to take her hurt away. To tell her that everything would be okay, but he would never be able to bring himself to lie to those deep brown eyes of hers that he had such an affinity for. Every day was a game of luck and calculated chance. While he knew that keeping her here with him was the most selfish thing that he could do, it was also the one thing that he wanted most.

"Erin-" Her voice was a broken cry, a soft plea. He'd never heard someone call for him so helplessly.

"I'm right here, Jewel." He reached a thumb out to smooth the wrinkle that had formed between her brows.

"Erin's here."

Then she opened her eyes halfway with some struggle, and he couldn't tell if the glassiness in them was from her tears or the fever. "I'm not a good idea." She warned.

"Just rest." Erin looked over her in concern. *She was talking out of her head again.*

The smallest whimper sounded in her throat, and she turned her head away from him and clenched her eyes shut to block the tears from spilling.

Oh darling.

Chapter Seventeen
Burn the Fine Line

"You didn't see anyone?" He asked, and Idalia curled into herself to try and preserve as much body heat as she could. Erin restricted her use of any blankets, but she wasn't quite sure that he understood just how frigid she felt.

"I thought you knocked, but it didn't sound like how you knock now that I think about it."

Erin rubbed a hand over his jaw, "And that was it, just the cup and the card?"

Idalia nodded and shivered simultaneously, and suddenly got the brilliant idea to stuff her feet as far underneath the material of her skirt as she possibly could.

Or it would have been a good plan if Erin hadn't caught her foot. "Don't break the rules, Jewel."

She cut him a light look, "We're living in a palace of villains, isn't this the one place I could break rules?"

An amused smile slid over his features, "Not when they're put in place for your good."

"Your heart is too kind for this situation." Idalia grumbled.

"Sorry, you're stuck with me as long as you want me around." He smiled gently.

"So, I'm never getting a blanket then." Idalia mumbled.

Erin paused and tilted his head, "Did you just say you want me around forever?"

"I've been poisoned, give me a break." She groaned and buried her face in the pillow.

Erin laughed for the first time that night, "Alright, noted." He glanced between her eyes and his expression became more somber, "You scared me, you know."

Idalia uncurled herself slightly so she could see him better. "I'm sorry." She replied, but there was a certain heaviness to her words that gave the impression that she was not just apologizing for one thing.

Erin tugged a hand through his messy hair, usually it looked so well-kept. "It wasn't your fault. Whoever drugged your drink however..." He didn't finish his sentence and Idalia had the suspicion that was because she already knew how he wished to end it. She could tell in that rapid flicker of a shadow that maneuvered in front of his caramel eyes.

"Their attempt failed; I only drank half of it."

"That's probably how you're still alive, Jewel."

"I just don't know who I've offended that would want to poi-" Idalia tapped her finger on her collarbone, "Correction, I don't know anyone here."

Erin stretched his back, "Oh... *Oh*." He furrowed his brow as the realization hit him. He exhaled and wrung his hand out, as if he was shaking invisible water droplets from his skin. He closed his eyes and clenched his fist before the tense muscles in his shoulders seemed to ease.

"What just happened?" Idalia asked curiously.

"Calliope. I should have known."

Idalia held her breath, "I knew she didn't like me, but I didn't know that it was enough to try and make me sick or worse." She let her gaze settle on the comforter, "Did she say something to you? I... saw you with her, the other day."

Erin's hand stilled from massaging his temple. "Oh, Jewel." He turned to her with a certain softness in his gaze. "I think you have that situation misconstrued."

Idalia fought another shiver, "I just couldn't see you two together, it doesn't make sense in my head."

Erin made a face, "Me and Calliope?" The thought seemed to absolutely appall him. "No, I was with her to help her get out of here. She..." He rotated a ring on his thumb, "I think you helped her realize that she was waiting for love from Lester, and I am quite sure that he is incapable."

"Oh..." Idalia curled back up into a ball again, perhaps to try and make herself small enough to hide from her assumptions.

"I would hope that you know me well enough to know that she is not my type." A warm chuckle trailed over his lips, clearly trying to put her at ease.

"Well, I mean we've never talked about it." A little smile pulled at her tired expression.

Erin's eyes glittered, "Okay that's fair." He tapped his fingers on his chin and then added.

"Brown eyes, lighter hair, a bit shorter than me, and a good heart."

Idalia lightly shook her finger in his direction before she shoved her hand back under the folds of her dress. "That's very incredibly broad, sir. Surely with those specifications you've seen somebody that fits that bill."

He flashed a smile, "And maybe I have. Now it's your turn."

"My turn for what?" She asked sleepily, her body was still fighting the effects of the poison she ingested.

"Your type."

Idalia rolled her eyes lightly. "Dark hair, dark eyes..." She mumbled thoughtfully, "I don't know if I've thought about superficial things more than that. If he's kind and loves me that's all I want."

Erin was quiet for a little while, and then she felt a gentle hand pressed against her forehead. "Your fever is coming down a bit. Do you think you can hold something on your stomach?"

She scrunched her nose but then relaxed the expression. It was a smart idea to eat something. "I'll try, but don't kick me out if I can't." A smidgen of playfulness laced her voice.

"I wouldn't dream of it, Jewel."

His hand rested on her forearm for a moment, and she felt the gentle graze of his fingertips along her sleeve before he eased off of the edge of her bed.

"Don't take any more suspicious deliveries until I get back." Erin gave her a pointed look but embellished it with a soft smile as he closed the door behind him.

She listened to his muffled footfalls echo down the quiet hallway and couldn't help replaying his words in her mind. While that description that he offered was quite vague, a ridiculous whisper in the back of her mind reminded her that underneath this protective guise that he crafted for her, she had those qualities.

Then she realized that he too, fit the description that she gave him.

Chapter Eighteen
Red Dresses and Cunning Eyes

Idalia had attended more balls in her time here than she'd ever dreamed of back in Thulta. Tonight, rich music filled the air. The burgundy material of her gown swished along the floor as Erin spun her around in sync with the other dancers.

"Who taught you how to dance?" He murmured close to her ear. He wanted to converse with her without prying eyes noticing his break in character.

"You're giving me too much credit, I'm just copying you." She whispered back, placing her jeweled shoe in the same vicinity that his own boot had been a few seconds before.

"You're doing a splendid job of fooling them." His lips curled upward as his hand shifted from her back to her waist as the dance required a dip.

A curl slipped out of her hairpin and dangled freely over her forehead. "You as well, my Prince." The same spark in her eye was mirrored by his own. It felt freeing and intrepid, and though the music roared to a crescendo, Idalia felt that glimmer drown out every other sound.

Only when Erin stopped swaying her as the song ended did she come back to reality. A herald dressed from head-to-toe in midnight black announced something that Idalia did not quite catch from their secluded position in the back of the ballroom.

Erin encapsulated her hand with his own as he led her forward. The attendees cleared a near instant path for them, and Lester beckoned for Erin to join him on the steps. He squeezed Idalia's hand so briefly that if anyone was looking, they wouldn't have noticed. She understood the silent message in it, though.

I'm still here. Don't worry.

"A kingdom is only as strong as those in support of it." Lester took his place on his gilded throne, and a malicious grin pulled his lips back from his teeth. "From where I sit, that strength is only growing."

A scattered cheer went through the crowd, and an overly excited guest drunkenly shoved into Idalia's arm as he raised his wine glass. The movement attracted the gazes of both Princes.

Erin's was one of concern.

Lester's, one of calculation.

Erin's brother said something to him, and Idalia saw him tense for a mere second before he stalked off the stairs and she lost sight of his form.

As she scanned the crowd, she was on guard as she felt an uneasiness roil in her gut. Who knew the horrors that these guests had committed? What separated them from those that Erin saved, were that these men and women refused to stop their crimes. They drew their energy from it and fed off each other's cruelty in a twisted alliance. The air felt thick, almost suffocating now that Erin was nowhere to be seen. Of course, she could fight if needed. But she could only take on two or three fully grown men at a time and she was in a corseted gown no less. Idalia became so engrossed in her strategy that she did not notice the royal brother who sauntered over to her, or the darkness that practically seeped in his wake.

"I fear that your date will be occupied for the rest of this evening." He murmured, and it raised alarm bells in

Idalia's mind. *She'd never heard him speak with such gentleness.*

"Then perhaps I should retire." She didn't hold his gaze for long, partly because she knew that looking too deeply into his eyes would reveal the monsters that he stored there.

"Perhaps." Lester allowed himself a generous look over her gown, and unfortunately, of her in it. When his gaze snagged on the small, beaded pearls that hug in swoops across her bodice, Idalia cleared her throat.

"Goodnight, your Majesty." She tipped her chin and backed away into the connecting hall. Her heartbeat thumped in her ears, and she realized too late that her heart was in fact, not that loud, but enhanced by the synchronized sound of heavy footsteps.

"I wasn't done with you, Pet." Lester cornered her, and Idalia did her best to swallow her fear. There was no one in the hallway, and on the off chance that a guest wandered through in their drunken stupor, they would certainly brush off the event because of his status.

"You intrigue me, I can see why my brother has taken an affinity towards you." The rings that adorned his own fingers caught on the satin of her sleeve.

Get away. Get away. "Thank you for the compliment." She swallowed, "But seeing as your brother... *saw* me first, I have to decline, this." Idalia felt her back press against the wainscotting on the wall, and Lester was not offering her much room to slip away.

Lester's eyes flicked down to her mouth.

"You could love me." He crooned, and Idalia could feel his own pulse in the fingertips that he used to graze her jaw. "Such a delicate thing." He murmured.

"I couldn't, it's not a choice." Her hand felt around the wall behind her back, for a ledge or anything that she could use as momentum to slip away from him.

"Isn't it?" Lester tilted his head, and she felt the heat of his lingering stare. Too warm. "I can offer you power. A *delicious* amount."

"That's a bribe." She shook her head in refusal.

"Don't women love power?" He asked thoughtfully.

"Sure, some do."

"So, in turn, you could love me." Lester smiled, and Idalia realized that if snakes could grin, they would resemble him.

"I said some, I didn't include myself in that category."

Something sharp and gleaming lit his dark eyes. "Pet, you could be queen someday. A big reward for small favors." Idalia felt a shudder creep up her spine at the fingers that he dragged along the side of her waist. She had to get out now.

"Is that what you told Calliope?" Idalia spat out once her fingers grasped the side of the wall and she took his moment of shock to pull herself out from under that lecherous gaze.

"I refuse to be like her."

Lester clenched his jaw and took a step towards her, so Idalia ran. She ran until she was breathless and every muscle in her legs burned as if they were being licked with flames. Idalia only stopped once her door was shut behind her.

When Erin came to look for her later that night, she said nothing and instead clung to him because she wanted to be embraced by arms that weren't out to hurt her. She wanted to feel that sense of safety that Erin always provided.

Erin rested his cheek on the top of her head and mumbled quiet words that were lost on her ears except for three of them.

"You're safe, Love."

Chapter Nineteen
Let Me Fix It, Won't You?

"Jewel, I need you to tell me what happened." Erin muttered into the quiet. He had held her for close to an hour, but Idalia was just now noticing how tense his body was against her. She unfurled her hands from his jacket and pulled away.

"I think you were adopted; I won't accept that you two are related."

Erin's jaw set, "Lester." He looked to the door as if pondering how quickly he could get to his brother. Then his gaze returned to her, "I'm so sorry." In the lackluster lighting, Idalia watched warring emotions swirl behind his eyes and the caramel shade darkened before he asked, "He didn't..." Erin's gaze dipped over her briefly, perhaps to check her for injury. "He didn't lay a hand on you, right?"

"Only my waist, although I don't want to know what he would have tried if I hadn't run." She admitted, and Erin's hand flexed on her forearm for a split moment.

"I need you to do me a favor and lay low for the next few days." Idalia found it puzzling that the tone of his voice sounded wildly different than what she was used to hearing. It sounded distant and taut.

"That's probably for the best."

Erin reached a hand out to her, but seemed to second-guess himself and he withdrew it. "Let me help you up." He gathered himself to his full height and pulled Idalia up with a careful grip. "No one should be treated like that; I know my apology doesn't help but-"

"No, it shows you care." Idalia interjected.

Erin's line of sight tracked to the side of the room, quietly deliberating something that was lost on Idalia, then the tension went out from his shoulders as he replied, "I do." He pulled her into his arms for a hug that felt like the most natural gesture in the world. They both stood at the ideal height for the embrace, she could rest her cheek against his inner shoulder, and his bowed head fit perfectly in the crook of her neck. The only sound in the room was that of the ticking clock in the corner, and it seemed like their heartbeats were settling in time to the makeshift metronome. Idalia tightened her arms around his chest once before they pulled away.

"Will I be in trouble for hugging a Prince?"

Erin gave a small chuckle, "It's probably the other way around, a criminal hugging a Sentry. The scandal."

Idalia pressed a light hand to her chest, feigning horror. "Think of the rumors."

That did not earn her one of his smiles that she had hoped for. There was still something lurking in Erin's expression. As if he wished to ruin his brother for laying a finger on her, while simultaneously keeping her tangled in his arms.

Idalia had to turn her face away at the thought.

She wouldn't mind that.

Chapter Twenty
Libraries and Reflections

I dalia had just finished writing her letter for tomorrow when she heard a thumping at her door. She had listened to Erin's request and had not left the safety of her room for the past few days. She tossed the scrap of paper onto the desk, which contained only two sentences.

I think we have this all wrong.

I'm done spying for you.

Idalia could no longer bring herself to write down the secrets that she heard murmured within these walls. She had yet to hear of any sort of war, and she wouldn't be able to live with herself if something happened to everything that Erin had worked for.

She would deliver the letter tonight. It would be the last one. Another thump echoed into her room, and she approached the mahogany door. That wasn't his normal knock, perhaps it wasn't Erin at all.

Then she heard, "It's me, my hands are full." A laugh intermingled with his voice. She bit back the smile that threatened to linger even after she unlatched the lock to let him in.

"What, did you raid the royal winery?" She raised her eyebrow at the glasses in his hands, filled with a fragrant burgundy.

He gave her a smile, "Of course not, I own the place remember?" Erin handed her a glass and took a seat on the couch closest to her instead of his usual favorite chaise.

"Ah yes, how could I forget." She dropped into a fake curtsy before she grabbed their deck of cards. "Couch or table?"

Erin moved so there would be an extra cushion in between them that would act as a surface for the game.

"This is fine."

"How was your day?" Idalia crossed her feet underneath her and shuffled the deck.

Erin swirled the wine in his glass, "Meetings and chores, boredom really. Nothing to concern your pretty head with."

She quirked an eyebrow at him. *He was kidding right?* He scanned over the cards in his hand and laid down too many. Idalia's brows furrowed, "Are you inventing new rules?"

Erin made a small noise in the back of his throat, "Ah, what can I say, I get rusty quite quickly." He swept the extra discarded ones back into his hand.

"You're trying to get me to let my guard down, so I underestimate you. Interesting tactic." Idalia clicked her tongue playfully and laid down a set.

"Have to keep things interesting, yes?" He gave her another smile and took a deep sip from the crystal.

"Perhaps I should adopt a new technique as well." Idalia rotated a card in between her fingers before she leaned to lay it down.

Erin's gaze snagged on the neckline of her dress, even lingering for a moment after she'd readjusted her posture. Idalia shifted uncomfortably on the cushion. Then he dropped his gaze back to his cards, "Did I tell you how lovely you look today?"

Idalia hesitantly drew a fresh card. "No... thank you though?" When their eyes met, Idalia noticed something that she hadn't before. His eyes were much darker.

"How many of those have you had tonight?" She jerked her chin to the glass he held. His lips pulled back from his teeth in a charming smile.

"Just one, perhaps my day was longer than I let on."

She'd never known Erin to be one to reach for the bottle when tensions were high. Perhaps she was just never around when he did.

They played for another half-hour, but after the fifth time she caught Erin's eyes wandering over her she snapped her fingers in his face.

"What's wrong with you today? I don't appreciate being looked at like this." Idalia wanted to fight the walls that tried to enclose her within them. He'd always been the perfect gentleman, what changed?

Erin blinked and then an apologetic note entered his voice, "I'm sorry, Idalia. I fear I'm not myself tonight."

She had the urge to grab a shawl and wrap it around her body like a cocoon. "I noticed." Her words were apprehensive, and that seemed to snap him out of whatever trance he had previously landed himself in.

"Can I make it up to you?" He settled a gentle hand on her own, and she felt the contrast between the warmth of his hand and the cold metal of his rings.

"Depends on whether or not you remember what manners are." Idalia gave him a light, scolding look.

Erin put his hand over his heart. "On my honor."

She seemed to consider it, "Alright, what do you have in mind?"

"I don't suppose you've ever seen the library." Something akin to mischief caught in his darkened eyes.

"I can't say that I have."

Erin haphazardly tossed the rest of his cards down and offered her his elbow when he stood. He seemed pleased when she took it, but didn't she always? Idalia brushed it off and let him lead the way.

The library was in the northern wing of the castle and hidden behind grand wooden doors that were adorned with black iron swirls. "My lady." He pushed a singular door open and gestured for her to walk in first.

Perhaps a touch of magic still lingered in this room, for when she set foot in the space, candles flickered to life and the light and shadows danced together in a harmonic duet. Rows upon shelves and a multitude of exorbitantly tall bookcases littered the space. There were rolling ladders attached to each one, and the scent of ink and leather-bound spines was intoxicating.

"My father had it commissioned for my mother, it was a wedding gift." Erin looked around, as if seeing the space through new eyes.

"She must have loved to read." Idalia ran her fingers over the line of books on the shelf closest to her. They had been immaculately kept, and no dust came away on her fingertips.

"She didn't have much time, helping to run this place and all." Erin appeared next to her and selected one of the books before casually flipping through the pages.

"I think she would be proud of you."

Erin stilled, his fingers hovering over the next page.

"You think so?" He closed the cover and slid it back onto the shelf amongst the others before he diverted his full attention to Idalia.

"I do." She murmured, and the bouncing candlelight softened his features, adding to the sense of warmth in his gaze.

"You're something special. Rare, even."

She chuckled, "I don't know about that, but thank you."

Somewhere between her last word and next breath, they'd moved closer to each other, to the point where she wouldn't have had to reach far to touch him.

Erin's hand tipped her chin up, with a sort of reverence that made something flutter in her stomach.

"I think you're beautiful." His words were soft, as if the both of them in this moment were a secret. He didn't have to be quiet, with only the books and the stories within them as their witnesses, but perhaps he was afraid to splinter away this moment.

His thumb brushed over her lips, and Idalia realized that if she were to lean in, even a fraction, he would kiss her.

Which... wasn't as startling of a realization as she thought it would be. Right before Idalia leant her head closer and eliminated the little gap between them, a cracking bang reverberated from the doorway.

"Get away from her." Erin growled.

Chapter Twenty-One
I Know You Aren't Mine

I dalia jolted backwards as she whipped her head from the man in front of her, to the one furiously stalking towards them. "Idalia, get behind me."

When she saw the way "Erin's" expression twisted, she was struck with an overwhelming sense of disgust. Although, it seemed that the real Erin felt this even more violently.

Erin slammed Lester into the bookshelf, causing some novels to tip over and smash into the floor in a flurry of bent covers and torn pages. "I won't tell you again." Sparks of fury ignited in the same eyes that were always so gentle with her, and he produced a dagger from what seemed to be thin air.

However, instead of holding the blade to Lester's throat, like Idalia thought he would, Erin pressed the point to Lester's wrist.

"You don't have it in you, little brother." Lester stared him down. A lesser man would have cowered underneath the intensity of that gaze, but Erin rotated the knife, drawing a prick of blood from Lester's skin and Idalia saw the other Prince tense.

Right before her eyes, Lester's face shifted from Erin's familiar features into his cold, harsh ones. Erin and Lester stood facing each other for another few moments. A deadly conversation wreathed in silence was taking place between the brothers, and it didn't seem that Erin was pleased with Lester's level of understanding. Finally, Lester shoved Erin back and left the library.

Idalia could still hear his footsteps echoing in the hallway even after he was gone. Yet, Erin remained firmly rooted in place.

Then he wiped the slight bit of crimson off his blade and slipped it back into the sheath at his hip. Erin rubbed a hand over his jaw and flexed his other one at his side.

"Are you okay?" The library suddenly felt very cold. *Had she truly almost kissed that monster?*

Erin's gaze drifted to her, the words he wished to say were on his tongue but his voice couldn't seem to comply. Instead, he shrugged off his jacket and draped it over her shoulders. He pulled the sleeves taut so the warmth would stay in place. "Come with me, please."

She followed close at his heels, and he kept glancing over his shoulder as if to make sure that she didn't get swept away by the shadows. "Where are we going?"

"Your room first." Was all the response that he gave.

When they got there, Idalia realized that Lester had left her door open. Perhaps he felt it was too bothersome to close it behind them.

"Grab whatever you need for tonight and tomorrow, I'll help."

"Am I going somewhere?"

Erin made a confirming noise, "I think it's best if you stay with me for the next little bit. You're not safe here anymore."

Idalia wanted to put his mind at ease, but that was a very difficult thing to do when she felt the same way. So, she nodded and proceeded to grab a few things and articles of clothing that she would need. Then she started folding a couple of the blankets.

"I've got blankets, Jewel." Erin's voice was beginning to soften again.

"I am not stealing your furs to make a pallet." She tried her hand at a half-chuckle, but it didn't sound quite right to her ears.

"You're insulting me if you really think I'm making you sleep on my floor." He gave her a sort of look that suggested that she rethink the apparent absurdity of her statement.

"Okay, then in that case I'm good to go." Idalia put the few items into a bag that Erin had dug out of her closet. *He must have put that there at one point.*

She hoisted the bag onto her shoulder, and he held the door open for her. "Do you want me to carry that for you?"

She shook her head, "I've got it, thank you though."

Erin lightly scoffed at himself, "I know you do, maybe I'm trying to make up for not being there tonight."

Idalia stepped in front of him, stopping him in his tracks, "That wasn't your fault." *It was hers.*

"Still." He offered her a small apologetic smile, but he fell silent for the rest of the walk to his quarters.

After they'd entered, he slipped the bag from her shoulder and put it up on his bed. "That's all yours."

"Erin-" Idalia started to refuse but he shook his head twice.

"Please, let me do this for you." He rubbed at the back of his neck, as if his guilt was manifesting into a spasm.

She hopped up on the luxurious mattress, "Thank you."

Erin dipped his chin in acknowledgement and unfastened her bag to put her things away.

She leant back against the headboard. "How could I have been so stupid." Idalia muttered under her breath, but the words weren't lost on him.

"Don't beat yourself up too badly, he's used that library trick before. However, his womanizing behaviors have officially hit too close to home." She saw his jaw clench.

"I just can't believe I almost kissed him." Idalia shuddered, and a wave of unease rolled over her at the thought.

"That surprised me too, what did he do that made you want to?" Erin hung up a smoky gray dress and then pulled her notebook out of the bottom of the bag.

Without thinking, Idalia replied, "I thought he was you."

The notebook fell right out of Erin's hands and slid underneath the dust ruffle.

Idalia and Erin both seemed to be trapped in a suspended state of staring at each other in shock.

"I'll get it!" She blurted, perhaps too emphatically. She moved off the mattress and reached under the bed.

Anything to hide her reddening face.

However, Erin apparently had the same idea and their hands found each other's instead of that pesky notebook. Their fingers stayed connected when they pulled them away from underneath the bed frame.

"I don't think I've ever seen you blush." He murmured, making absolutely no moves to unwind their hands.

Idalia would have felt embarrassed if she hadn't noticed the exact same coloring blooming across his own features. "You are too."

He brushed the side of his face with his hand, and clearly it came away feeling the warmth. "That's... a first." Then his eyes widened some, as if he hadn't meant to say that out loud.

"I think we should um," Idalia slipped her hand away and stood up.

"Try and get some rest." He offered and clasped his hands behind his back. "Good idea."

She scrambled back onto the bed and drew her legs close to her chest. Erin flicked the light off and she heard him shuffle around before he eased down onto a chaise that was quite like the one in her room. *Maybe that's why he always went for that one.*

Then Idalia's mind wandered. She should have known something was amiss. Lester had given her plenty of hints, and she felt bad that she had blamed Erin when it was merely Lester wearing his appearance.

"I'm sorry." She mumbled into the dark.

Cloth rustled from the corner of the room; he was probably rolling onto his side. "For what, Jewel?"

"I should have known better. You would have never said or done the things that he did. I-" *Oh, there was so much she wanted to say, why was it this hard to find the words?*

"The fact that you trust me enough to believe an impression of me, speaks volumes. Tonight, was entirely his fault." He was quiet for a minute. "I'm sick of people using you. You've had enough of that in your old life, and you don't need it again."

Idalia was thankful that the lights were off, so he couldn't see the mist that was gathering at her lash line.

"Thank you."

"Always."

Chapter Twenty-Two
Monsters Lurk in the Dark

I dalia woke herself up with a start when she realized that she had not delivered her final letter. Sure, she'd swiped it off her desk when Erin told her to collect her things, but their last conversation filled her mind to the point that she had thought of nothing else. Now the issue would be to get it out of the notebook that still lay under the bed, without waking up her Prince.

Her Prince? No, what was she thinking?

Erin. Without waking up Erin.

She eased out of bed and carefully dropped to her knees to scavenge for the misplaced book. Her fingernails dug into the cover, and she slid it across the floor, wincing at the slight scraping noise that the binding produced as it moved.

Erin didn't seem to stir. Idalia rose to her feet and plucked the envelope free of the pages. Before she exited, she spared a look over her shoulder to where he rested. The moonlight and shadows that danced over his features from the curtained window made him look so unguarded, so peaceful. He wasn't the villain everyone made him out to be.

One more letter, he'd still be safe.

Dirt accumulated underneath Idalia's nails as she readjusted the rock atop the envelope. It felt as if lead chains had been lifted from her chest, and when she looked up at the burning stars, Idalia breathed deeply. No more spying, no more secrets. At least, not from Erin.

Idalia exhaled slowly and drank in her surroundings. Despite it being the middle of the night, this place no longer seemed so frightening. She could see herself being happy to stay here. After all, if she were to crave lush grass under her feet instead of these blackened blades, they had Sylvie's Oasis. If she was homesick, she had no doubt that Erin would sneak her out for a while. Perhaps one day she could even ask to help him with the reformation program. With a comforting sense of certainty, she crept back into the palace.

She had to catch herself from walking down the hallway that led to her old room. Perhaps it was paranoia from earlier this night, but she had a strange sense that the shadows from that eerie hallway would latch onto her ankles were she to linger for long.

The door to his quarters clicked softly shut, but when her eyes landed on his chaise, the sigh of relief at not having woken him up vanished from her lungs. *He wasn't there.*

Surely, Lester wouldn't have summoned him at this hour. Even serpents had to sleep at some point.

Idalia waited a moment for her eyes to adjust to the pale light of the moon. "Erin?" She whispered, feeling her way around the wrought iron bedposts. Then her eyes snagged on a quiver of movement in the corner in front of the adjacent window. He had his back turned to her, and she could tell by his outline that he had cast aside his tailored jacket. "Erin?" Her voice was less hushed this time. *Why wasn't he responding to her?*

She took light steps in his direction, but her foot made contact with his discarded jacket, and the gilded buttons raked over the marble floor.

"Just one kill to prove it." He finally spoke, and Idalia's body tensed. *His voice sounded... wrong.* Almost as if he was parroting words from a past darkness. "But one becomes two, and after that, who's counting?" Erin pressed the face of his palm against the glass of his window, peering out into the murky gardens below. Watching, but not quite. Seeing, but blindly.

"Erin." Idalia reached out her hand and grazed his shoulder. Even through the fabric of his shirt she could tell the skin underneath was cold. While she had noticed that his body temperature seemed to run cooler, this was a drastic difference.

He very slowly tore his gaze from the window to the light hand on his arm. "A puppet." Erin said thoughtfully, and every word out of his mouth was slowly articulated. "I choke them with my strings."

He wasn't blinking.

Because he wasn't awake.

"Hey." She slipped her hands into his unfeeling ones. "Let's get you to lie down."

Erin didn't fight, but before she managed to get him to lean back onto the chaise, he lifted his gaze to her. "I found her mama; I found the one you told me about." His words were almost mumbled, but then Idalia noticed that some of the tension dissipated from his shoulders as she eased him down.

"Just rest." Idalia soothed. When she stole the throw from his bed to drape over his form, her stomach twisted as she saw his expression shift into one of pain. *What had he meant when he said that he choked them with his strings?*

Erin kept shifting in his fitless sleep, and Idalia decided that she wouldn't leave him. He may not have been awake, but he wouldn't be alone. Idalia sat down on the rug and drew her legs to her chest. The clock in his room ticked by with gentle clicks. Marking the minutes that slipped past her fingertips. Somewhere after the seven thousandth tick, her head gravitated towards the wooden and glass table, cushioned by her arm. She'd close her eyes for a moment.

Just one moment.

Chapter Twenty-Three
Not Just a Symbol

I dalia was pulled from her sleep by the sensation of gentle fingertips on her cheek. There was a softness to the touch, reminiscent of how one would trace the delicate wings of a little bird.

"You okay, Jewel?"

Idalia peeked one eye open. His voice sounded different in the early morning than she was used to. Like a rough tumbled stone instead of a polished one. "Yes, why?"

Erin's mouth curled in amusement and his gaze purposely flicked from her to the grand bed to their left. "Well, you're using my table as a pillow."

She smoothed her hair back and became aware of the muscle spasm that had tightened in her neck from the angle that she slept. "Didn't want you to be alone." Idalia yawned.

Erin tilted his head, and his sleep tousled bangs slid over one of his eyes. "If you missed me, you could have just said so," he teased. But then she felt his hand pull her hair behind her shoulder before he massaged the ache in it with a pleasant pressure.

"You're much more alert than you should be this early."

"Occupational hazard, I'm afraid." Erin chuckled warmly, moving his attention to the muscle on the opposing side of the spasm. When his hand rested over her skin, Idalia felt the chill of his rings and jumped, a shiver crawling over her arms.

Erin immediately jerked his hands back, "Did I hurt you?"

Idalia turned her head back to look at him, "What? Oh no, your rings were cold."

There was a relieved light that entered his eyes,

"Good." She then watched as he slipped every ring off except for the one on his left ring finger.

"Hold these for me, please?" He dropped them all unceremoniously into her waiting palm.

"I don't think I've ever seen you take these off." She prodded the metal bands and turned some of them over. They were so incredibly detailed, but she had never paid much attention.

"That's because I never do. There's sentimental value in each one, but don't tattle on me. I'm supposed to be scary, not have an affinity for jewelry." Erin leant down closer to her as if sharing a secret.

"What does this one mean to you?" Idalia held a blackened ring with the design of a roaring lion up to the sunlight that poured into the room.

Without skipping a beat on massaging her shoulder, he replied, "Old family crest. Mother helped craft it, but when Lester took over, he did away with it."

"I like it." Idalia nodded, "This one?" She brushed her fingertips over a thinner band. Onyx black, with swirls running through the design.

"Twentieth birthday present. Mama Rose and a few others from the house pulled their money together and surprised me." She heard the smile in his voice as he recollected the memory. "So naturally, I've worn it for the past four years."

Idalia leant her head back once more with a teasing grin, "I just realized I'm a year older than you."

"You sure? Your height suggests otherwise."

"Sir, I will steal one of these rings if you keep on." Idalia cut him a playful glare.

Erin laughed, "Jewel, that'd fall right off of your finger."

"Fine. You can make it up to me by telling me about this one." Idalia plucked the golden band that he usually wore on his thumb and rolled it between her fingers.

"That actually wasn't meant to be a ring. My mother wore it on a chain. A few months after she passed, I went through some of her things and found it."

Idalia ran her thumb over the delicately engraved design. Tiny, golden roses roped around the metal if one looked closely enough. "I wish I could have met her."

Erin's hand paused on her neck. "Me too, Jewel."

"We could have sassed you together." Idalia added light-heartedly after hearing the somber note in his voice.

Erin snickered, "I think just you doing it is all I can handle."

A soft laugh left her, "And this one?" She reached her fingertips behind her to settle over his left hand, landing on the dark ring that he still wore, the one with a single ruby fastened into its middle.

"Ah, that one's sentimental for a different reason." Erin rested his forearm on her shoulder so Idalia could see his hand without having to crane her neck. "Purity ring."

Idalia quirked an eyebrow, "What does that mean?"

Erin flexed his hand, making the ruby catch in the light. "It's a symbolic reminder, of a choice I made a long time ago." He responded thoughtfully, "I want the only person to *know* me in that way to be the girl I marry."

Idalia traced over the ring, "She'll be incredibly lucky." She murmured to herself. Then more loudly she added, "I have the same belief, I just never knew there was a symbol for it." Idalia glanced down at her unadorned ring finger.

Then she felt Erin's hands shift to the thin necklace chain around her neck. He unhooked the latch and it trailed from her neck. "Hmm..." He hummed and slipped his golden band from her palm before threading it through the metal.

To her surprise, he refastened the necklace, and his ring rested at her collarbone with a gentle weight. She closed her hand over it, "Erin, I can't take this. It belonged to your mama. I was joking before about stealing one." Idalia made a move to take the necklace off, but Erin caught her hand.

"I want you to have it, Jewel. Besides, now I won't be the only one here with morals." A melodic laugh left his lips, and Idalia felt her heart tumble over.

"Thank you. You'll tell me if you want it back, right?"

Erin gathered her long locks and placed them where they had rested before, "I don't go back on my gifts, sweet one." He stood to his feet and extended his hand to Idalia.

She let him pull her up, but she didn't ease her hand out from his careful grip. Was it just her, or did his eyes have a certain new shimmer to them? They were the type of honeyed caramel that was so incredibly easy to get pulled into with their warmth and light. *Like a fire that would never burn her.*

"Do I have something on me?" Erin chuckled as he rubbed a hand over his jaw.

She'd been staring. "No-" Idalia said quickly. "Sorry, I got distracted." She let his hand be, returning her own to her side.

Erin folded his arms and leant back against the wall, a playful look on his face. "Ah, yes, I bet my bed hair is very charming." For emphasis he shook his head to make the layers even messier.

"Oh, you missed a piece." Her lips curled and she reached up to tug her hand through his bangs, flipping them to the side. "Gorgeous."

"Mm, I doubt that." Erin raised his eyebrow but leant his head into her touch the smallest bit, as if testing to see if she'd drop her hand or keep it there.

She kept it there.

Erin opened and closed his mouth, as if trying to figure out how to formulate the words in his head. "You don't... treat your other friends this way, do you." It was less of a question and more of a hesitant statement, but there was a certain note of longing in it that she almost didn't catch.

"No." Idalia murmured, "But they never treated me the way you do."

Erin made a small acknowledging noise, but then he cleared his throat and pushed off the wall. "I should prob-ably-" He took a step backwards, but his eyes were still locked on hers, so he nearly collided with the bedpost.

"Get ready?" Idalia offered as she tried to fight the smile that was dying to appear.

"Yes. That. Thank you." Erin looked from her to the piece of furniture that seemingly had it out for him. Then he slipped off into the other room.

Idalia covered her mouth to stifle a little laugh. Perhaps she wasn't the only one who'd been distracted this morn-ing, although she knew how absurd even entertaining the thought was. Then some inner part of her heart filled her mind with hypotheticals. What was the harm in secretly replaying the last few moments in her mind? Surely nothing could come from memorizing that feeling of his fingertips on her cheek, or the gentleness in his gaze...every time he looked at her.

Idalia sighed. There *was* harm in it, because she could tug on these threads and see where they may lead, and she could slip and tumble until she fell. But would that be so horrible if he were to catch her?

Then her mind happened upon something that she hadn't previously realized: *What if he already had?*

The Murmur

She held this wondrous spark in her eyes. Child-like, in a sense. The things that she had been through in the past weighed on her shoulders like invisible lead chains, but she never allowed them to touch that dancing flame.

That little spark always did seem to light when she was happy.

So, it became a desire of my heart to see just how happy I could make her.

Chapter Twenty-Four
The Cards He Was Dealt

"Question for you." Erin re-entered the room after several hours of tending to whatever chores Lester had tasked him with.

"I may or may not have an answer." Idalia snickered as she tore out a page in her notebook and crumpled the paper into a haphazard ball.

Erin shook his head in amusement, "You're welcome to stay here, but I'll be gone for the rest of the night. I'm on dungeon duty."

"So, your question is?" Idalia quipped.

"Oh, right." Erin rubbed the back of his neck, "Did you want to tag along? I get it if you'd prefer not to, but I also hate having you holed up in this room. I'd get stir crazy pretty fast." He was rambling and seemed to notice it with a slightly confused draw of his brows.

Idalia smiled, "I'd love the company." She stretched and joined him at the door. "The dungeon, isn't that where I was supposed to end up a few months ago?"

Erin flicked up his brow, "Don't jinx us, we're flirting with danger enough as it is."

"At this point I'm practically engaged to it."

"Tsk, I didn't even get a wedding invite."

Idalia shook her head, "So what exactly is, 'dungeon duty?'"

Now that they were out in the hallway amongst possible listening ears, all he replied was, "multitasking," with a quick glance that explained the situation further. Idalia couldn't help but wonder what it must have been like to grow up in this place. If someone set her loose with a blindfold, she had no doubt that she would get more turned around than a tangled ball of yarn. Yet, Erin's steps were sure and filled with a sense of steadiness that never seemed to waver.

The entrance to the dungeon was in the very heart of the castle. It was quite literally a gaping void of darkness, a hole in the floor with stairs that spiraled down like a hazardous vortex.

Erin's polished boots touched down on the first step and then the second, before he realized that he did not hear Idalia's footsteps behind him. He turned and glanced at her quizzically, "Everything alright?"

Idalia peered further into the expanding abyss and squinted. "How can you see where you're going?"

Erin glanced down into the plunging cavity and then back to the light, "Oh, I'm sorry Jewel. I'm a creature of habit." His lips curled in the way that she knew meant he wanted to give her his real smile, but pretenses were crucial here. She'd learned that more than anything.

However, he disappeared from her sight for the next couple of minutes, before she heard his footfalls once more and, in his hand, was a bronze lantern.

"Is night-vision one of your gifts?"

"I think it's more enhanced than typical. Nature's way of making up for living in a place where everything is dark and darker." He shrugged one shoulder and then pulled a match from his pocket and struck it against the side of the stone wall.

"Watch your step, it can be slippery down here." Erin warned as he set the lantern ablaze.

Idalia gathered up the skirts of her dress with one hand as they descended. She wasn't quite sure what to expect. The other Sentries used to gather and tell fictitious stories of the Gate's prison, but she had never paid them much mind. After all, who would have known that someday she'd be crossing over to the heart of it while having the utmost assurance that her life would remain intact.

The stairs curved downward into this seemingly bottomless pit, but she knew that they were getting closer when an overwhelming sulfuric stench permeated her nostrils. It smelled of rotting rats and decayed hope. Idalia's hand covered her nose to keep from gagging, a motion that Erin's eyes tracked quickly. He pulled the pocket square out of his jacket, flicking the cloth until it was unfolded and gently held it to her nose.

Thank the Author. Idalia breathed deeply, and her brain recognized the overly pleasant scent. She'd caught a whiff of it the night that they had embraced. The combination of crackling firewood and spiced cider was so unique to him.

"This smells like you." Her voice was mumbled by the cloth. The lantern light reflected in Erin's eyes as he glanced over to her.

"Who knew you were a fan of cologne?" Idalia heard the teasing in his murmured tone, but as she was about to offer a playful retort, the grating sound of dragging chains filled her ears with a metallic screech.

"Gardner, Phinn." Erin's voice morphed into something so commanding, and Idalia doubted that the two guards he referred to had ever heard their names uttered with such power.

"Prince." They both instantly dropped down to a knee. However, the guard on the left continued to clutch the shackles attached to a gaunt-looking prisoner.

"I had some time on my hands," Erin said coolly, "you're relieved of your rotation." He showed his open palm, awaiting the chains, with the expectancy of one who was used to having everything handed to him without question.

How wrong that assumption was, Idalia thought. *Even this flawless façade required work.*

"My Prince, forgive us, but his Highn-"

Erin's hand never wavered, "*I* said you're relieved. Or have you forgotten that the prison is under my domain, not my brother's?"

It amazed Idalia that two guards of the Gate with broad frames that rivaled Erin's own, were practically quivering with the fearful anticipation of what threatening promise could lie in the Prince's words.

"Of course, your Highness." The bolder guard handed over the chains. "Would you like us to return the lady to her quarters?" The guard, Phinn, had a hand hovering close to Idalia's arm, ready to proceed with the order upon command.

Erin sighed, but there was nothing defeated in the exhale, only disturbance with a tinge of annoyance. "Idalia darling, it's your choice."

There was a minute, subtle inflection that changed in his voice when Erin flicked his gaze back to her. Was it intentional or just the sense of familiarity that they had with each other that allowed her to catch it?

"I'd like to stay." She replied, moving the sweetly scented cloth from her face. If she breathed shallowly, the foul-smelling air was slightly more tolerable. Erin flicked his wrist to dismiss the two other men.

The echo of heavy boots thumped behind them and then dissipated, leaving Erin and Idalia alone. As alone as one can be in a dungeon filled with the worst Thulta had to offer.

"I'd leave him if I were you." The older female prisoner who was bound by the shackles croaked. Her voice sounded like someone had reached into her throat and punched holes in her vocal cords. It sent a strange shiver down Idalia's back, but she didn't show it. "Royal snake." The woman spat at Erin's feet, and Idalia had the sudden urge to shove both the prisoner, and her accusations backwards.

Erin led the woman to an uninhabited cell. Much like the style of the main Gate, the cell doors curved with sharp iron in a way that would break the skin quite gruesomely should one grab a hold of it.

"I'm not afraid to die, if that's what you're planning." The woman tried to yank her bound wrists from Erin's hold.

"What I am planning, is none of your concern right now." Erin tightened his grip on the shackles and backed the prisoner into her new home for the foreseeable future.

"He'll leave you, kid." Her raspy voice was now directed at Idalia, "Men like him only want one thing and then it's-" She made a whistling noise which highlighted one of her missing teeth, and jerked her thumb backwards, making the chains rattle.

Crazy old crone. Idalia held her tongue, although she wished to berate the woman for not realizing how lucky she was to have been placed here under Erin's guard instead of Lester's.

"Idalia is a free woman. She knows she can leave if she wishes." Erin turned a dark gray key into the door's lock, and right as he turned on his heel, Idalia caught a flicker of a stolen glance from him.

The woman sidled as close to the iron cell door as she could without her skin tearing and scoffed. "Probably will use you for heirs."

A disgusted huff left Idalia, and she took a step towards the bitter woman right as her arm started to tingle with that sensation that she'd only experienced once before. A quick glance at her forearm revealed hastily scribbled cursive in a deep sable ink.

Don't pay her any mind, Jewel.

Idalia drew a controlled inhale and followed Erin who had started down the adjacent corridor of the underground prison. Both sides of the walls had cells carved into them, and she felt eyes on her back as they passed. A rat sprinted from underneath one door, and became tangled in her skirts, squeaking violently. The prisoner in the cell to their left roared with laughter.

"Can't handle a teensy-weensy mouse, girlie?"

Idalia had dealt with way too many rodents in the past to be made a laughingstock because one became entrapped in the folds of her dress. Erin had started to kneel to fish the little creature out, but she promptly bent, separated the fabric from the rat, and captured it in two hands. It squirmed and thrashed, trying to make an escape. "He's kind of cute, all things considered." Idalia adopted a shyer tone and tossed the rodent with perfect calculation through the swirl in the door. Straight onto the snarky man's chest.

"Oops, he jumped." She said innocently. Erin cleared his throat to mask a laugh as the male prisoner shuddered and flung the rat from his body, before glowering at Idalia.

"Erin, we get that you have a bleeding heart, but this girlfriend of yours is a menace." The man grumbled.

The caramel-eyed Prince leant against the wall that supported a torch and folded his arms. "She'll probably throw another one at you for being so presumptuous, Matthias."

"Hopefully she's got the common sense to not get involved with the likes of you." He raised an eyebrow, but then a chuckle rumbled from his chest.

"You..." Idalia's shoulders dropped a touch, "know each other don't you."

"I was about to introduce you but then you know, the rat." Erin smirked.

"Funny." She gave him a look, then turned to the man. "Sorry for that."

Matthias rolled his shoulder, as if shrugging off the moment entirely. "Good arm on you. Archer?" He asked.

"It feels like a lifetime ago." Idalia offered a slight smile, and her words piqued Erin's interest.

"I didn't know that." He murmured to her.

"What, did you think I was only skilled in shard fighting?" She leant closer to him in her tease.

"No, you are a woman of many talents, as you often remind me." Erin slid her an easy grin, also inclining his head towards hers.

Matthias snapped his thick fingers. "Hey Romeo and Juliet, are you here for a reason or is this a new odd punishment, making me watch this."

Erin rolled his eyes, "A little friendly banter and suddenly he's nauseous."

"We've got different definitions of friendly, Shifter-boy." Matthias slumped down against the wall.

"I'll be nice." Erin threw his hands up in surrender, but not before giving Idalia a quick wink. Then he crouched next to the cell door, "I came here to check up on you."

Matthias flexed both of his hands, "I'm getting by."

"Have you thought about what I said?" Erin questioned gently. It was the type of softness that made Idalia want to curl up with his words like a blanket.

"I just don't think I'm ready for it. Yet." Matthias tacked on. "There's too much I need to sort through up here." He tapped a meaty finger to his forehead.

"I understand that, believe me. I do." Erin sat down amongst the dirt and grit of the floor and rested his elbow on a raised knee. "But anything you've done in the past is going to stay in the past. You don't go digging up a body that's already been buried."

"You do if you're a grave robber." Matthias reasoned with the raise of his bushy brow.

Erin chuckled, "True, but you could start fresh. Find a good job, maybe even a sweet girl to come home to?"

Idalia could tell that Erin would have nudged Matthias's shoulder in jest if the iron hadn't divided them.

A rumble sounded from Matthias's chest, a sort of grunt and laugh mingled together. "I'd kind of given up on the whole 'hopes for the future' thing." He swatted away a piece of hay that had drifted from the makeshift pile of bedding in the corner. "Do you really think it could work?" Matthias's tone became smaller, more unsure.

"I think you'll beat yourself up if you don't try. Besides, I'm getting tired of seeing your burly mug down here." Erin nodded to playfully confirm his words, and Matthias tipped his head back and laughed.

"We'll see." Matthias appeased him, and then his gaze caught on Idalia as she moved to sit down in front of Erin.

"What's your story, then, Lass?"

Idalia darted a glance to Erin, for a look of encouragement or disapproval. While it seemed that he knew this man, she wasn't sure if it was fully genuine or if it was another extension of his act. Erin only rested his chin on his inclined knee, quietly awaiting her answer.

"Well," Idalia smoothed out the folds in her skirt, "I'm afraid it's not that noteworthy of a past, my earliest memories are from the orphanage I grew up in-"

"Miss Sarah's?" Matthias suddenly interjected.

Idalia tilted her head, "Yes, how did you know?"

Matthias made a noise in the back of his throat, "I was there for a good while, back when she'd first opened the place."

Idalia felt a new sense of connection to this man, albeit they were strangers, but there was now a link to their histories. "I never met Sarah, and I never paid much attention to the adults that would come by. Except..." Idalia trailed off, and her gaze tracked to the side, past Erin's head. Clearly lost in thought.

"Yes?" Erin was the one to softly bring her back.

"Well, it sounds silly now, but-" Idalia drew her legs to her chest and interlocked her fingers around her knees. "I ran away when I was about eight. It was getting dark, and I got lost. There was this kind woman, I recall... She found me. She gave me a white flower and led me back." Idalia gave a small chuckle, "I remember thinking, whoever had her as a mother was so very lucky." Idalia rolled her thumb and index finger together, as if recalling the texture of that flower's stem.

"You can find family in the most unlikely places." Matthias responded, with a hint of reminiscence in his voice. As if her story was bringing back memories of his own.

"Most unlikely meetings too." Erin muttered so quietly, it was a wonder Idalia heard him. He'd stolen a glance at her, and now his gaze settled on his rings.

"So, after that you picked up a bow and arrow?" Matthias's chuckle reverberated through the dingy hall.

"Not quite, but when I was younger there was a traveling archer. It was pure happenstance that we met, but I'd been practicing aiming at a scrawny tree and according to him, I had the 'skills of a blind squirrel.'"

"Oh my." Erin snickered, "I do have to admit your aim has definitely improved, Jewel."

An amused smile tugged on her rouged lips, "I used the tips he gave me, and then kept on practicing until I was good enough to become a Sentry."

Matthias raised both eyebrows at Erin. "Well, it's been nice knowing you, she'll probably turn you in for coin." A smirk played on his unshaven features.

"Tomorrow." Idalia suppressed a grin and leaned her head back against the wall, watching the flash of a sparkle in Erin's eyes as she repeated the word that he'd told her many times before.

Suddenly, the large bell in the courtyard above clanged loudly to announce the arrival of midnight. *They'd been here for that long?*

"You'd better go, before you turn into a pumpkin or whatever it is that royalty does." Matthias's gruff voice held an almost compassionate note to it. As Idalia and Erin rose to their feet, Matthias did as well.

"Hey Erin? I'll keep thinking about it." Matthias affirmed, and Erin dipped his chin in hopeful acknowledgment.

Then they left, heading for the absurd number of winding stairs. When her footing faltered, he was right there to catch her, before leading them both out into the open air.

"So, tomorrow huh?" Erin's lips curved, and held his wrists out in jest, as if she would cuff them for an arrest.

Idalia merely placed her hands on top of his. "It's a strange thing, that 'tomorrow' never does seem to come."

"Very strange." He agreed.

The Murmur

I had always thought that when someone found their person, there would be an instantaneous sign, like a clap of thunder or a strike of lightning. However, my realization was instead that of an ocean wave. Slowly growing and curling and curving until it crashed over me, and I had no choice but to surrender to it completely as it swept me away.

I had never been so happy to drown.

Chapter Twenty-Five
Dirt and Danger

E rin and Idalia slipped away into the back garden instead of returning to their quarters. "Somehow even air so stale smells better than the prison."

Idalia nodded, letting her eyes close to savor the slight breeze that carried over her shoulders. "It is a little stale, but I like to think I've gotten used to it."

Erin quirked a brow, "Alright Jewel, I think the dungeon's stench has gotten to you."

"I'm serious." She chuckled and walked around in the garden. "I wonder if one day we can plant some flowers out here, some shrubbery that isn't," she plucked a leaf from a rotting bush, and it crumpled to pieces almost instantly, "dusty." She finished.

Erin cocked his head, "Sounds like you're making some long-term plans."

Idalia wiped the brittle leaf fragments from her fingers onto her skirt. "Oh- sorry, I just thought..."

"Are you wanting to stay?" Erin asked, and then more quietly he tacked on, "For good?"

Idalia nudged the dirt with the toe of her boot. "Do you want me to?"

Something in Erin's expression shifted, but before she could tell if it was a good change or a bad one, she noticed a problem. The stone that she had placed her final letter under was still untouched. The leaves and caked mud around it had dried and formed a seal since the last rain. Idalia went to it and pried the rock loose. Her letter was falling apart. The moisture had caused the writing to bleed through to the envelope to the point that she was certain it wouldn't be legible anymore.

Trevor never came for the letter.

Something was wrong.

"Idalia?" Erin slowly approached from behind her, "What is it?"

Idalia plucked the letter from the ground. "I have to leave."

Chapter Twenty-Six
Don't Say Goodbye

"What do you mean?" Erin looked confused and alarmed all at once.

"Come on." Idalia motioned for him to follow her, and she didn't speak until the door to his chambers was bolted. "Something's not right." She paced the length of his ornate rug. "I left this, it said I wasn't going to be a spy for them anymore, and no one has taken it."

Erin held the dilapidated envelope up to the lamplight and frowned, "So, what are you saying?"

"I'm saying I don't trust how their minds work. I need to talk to Trevor." Idalia mumbled as she racked her brain.

Erin gently tugged her hand away before she ripped the skin, "Do you need to leave tonight?"

Idalia nodded, "It's not sitting right with me."

"Alright, then let's go." Erin turned towards the door, but Idalia caught his sleeve.

"Wait-" She blurted, "You're coming with me?"

Erin paused, "I told you before to trust that I wouldn't say goodbye. I'm not going to leave you."

Idalia's grip slackened on his sleeve. He had everything a man could want. Yet, he looked at her like she was his greatest treasure. She'd scold herself for this later, but she wished that she was.

"Thank you." She whispered.

Chapter Twenty-Seven
Old Friends, New Hearts

The singular lantern that offered a smidgen of illumination to the compound's door swung back and forth in the gusts of wind. It was jarringly quiet, but Idalia figured it was because of the unholy hour in which they'd crept into Thulta. She rapped on the door. *Twice, then once more.*

"Maybe they're asleep?" Erin whispered from her left while continually glancing over his shoulder to their surroundings.

"Sentries sleep light." Idalia knocked on the door more forcefully. Then she heard bolts slide out of position from the inside before the door swung open to reveal a very haggard looking Trevor. He had rings underneath his eyes that were tinged in blue and an ashy purple. "Dilly?" Trevor scrubbed at his tired face, "And... Keir?"

"I need to talk to you, now." Idalia took a step closer to the door, and Trevor stepped backwards to hold the door open wider for them.

"Oh- Come in." Trevor ushered the pair in, and then added, "Now what's this about?"

"Why did you not come for my last let-"

"Idalia." Trevor warned, as his eyes darted to Erin. "Perhaps we should speak in private." He beckoned for her to follow him before addressing Erin, "Sorry, surely you understand."

Erin seemed to be surveying Trevor. "Of course, you never can be too careful nowadays."

Idalia spared the disguised Prince one more glance before she followed Trevor alone. The lock clicked on the meeting room door. It sounded eerily like the ticking of a clock, reminding her of the time that she could be losing.

"My letter, how come you never came for it?"

Trevor looked her over, "There's been a change of plans."

Idalia's nails scraped against the flesh of her palm as she tightened her fist. "You didn't feel the need to inform me of this because?"

"I was going to, but-" Trevor tugged a hand through his tawny hair, "I wasn't sure if it was safe."

Idalia wanted to ask him since when had he cared about safety, but she swallowed the words. "What change in plans, exactly?"

Trevor hesitated, "I'm... not at full liberty to discuss that right now."

Idalia wanted to shake him. "You're kidding."

Trevor held his hands up in surrender. "Mox went with half of the Sentries to Esterod, they'll be back within the week, and they can fill you in."

"You could fill me in right now." Idalia pressed.

"Dilly-Dally, you know protocol. On the off chance that you've been compromised, we can't risk a Gate invasion with the majority of our Sentries away."

Idalia clenched her jaw so hard that she felt it pop. "I need you to listen to me, I think we've got the wrong idea about what's happening there."

Trevor furrowed his brows, "That's not what you've reported."

"I need you to trust me. Tell Mox and the others to hold off on whatever it is their planning."

"Dilly, you're not making sense. If it's this important, tell them yourself in a few days."

Idalia rubbed her temples in frustration, and Trevor softened his voice. "How have you been?"

"How I am is not important-"

"It is to me." Trevor reached for her hand. The touch felt strangely different from Erin's. Trevor's was rougher and more demanding, even at his gentlest.

"Listen, I'm sorry I haven't been able to protect you from that place. Your time away has really made me think."

"I don't need your protection; I need you to shut up and listen to me." Idalia blew a black wavy curl from her face.

"There's been no talk of any war, and I have lived there for months!" She exclaimed.

Trevor's hands found her shoulders. "Be honest with me, have they bribed you?"

Idalia balked, "Where on earth would you get that idea?"

Trevor's gaze purposely darted down to the beautifully crafted golden band that now hung at her collarbone. *A jewel fit for a Prince.*

Idalia pushed him backwards with her palm. "You son of a pig." She scoffed in disbelief, "We'll see what the others have to say about this." Idalia turned and settled her hand on the doorknob. "I just wish that for once, you'd take me seriously." Her words lingered in the air long after she'd departed from the room.

"Hey, what's the verdict?" Erin questioned quietly, pulling his form away from the wall he'd been leaning on.

Idalia grabbed his hand and dragged him outside into the windy night and behind the compound. "He won't tell me until the others are here."

"How long will that take?" His voice was low, yet the breeze carried every syllable to her ears.

"According to that genius in there, a week." Idalia pinched the bridge of her nose.

"Okay, then we'll-"

"No." She interrupted, "You can't be gone that long." Idalia softened her tone, "A day or two is different than a week, and I can't risk not being here if they arrive early."

Erin's gaze tracked to the wall behind her, seemingly searching each crevice in the rock for a loophole to her response. Seeing that he was struggling to find one, she added; "This is my mess that I got us into, I need to be the one to fix it."

"This mess involves both of us, Jewel. I can-"

Idalia cut off his speech by wrapping her arms around his neck and holding him close. Erin was stunned for a moment before his arms encircled her. "Leave a Gate open for me, okay?" She mumbled into the collar of his cloak.

"You really are engaged to danger." It sounded as if he tried to chuckle, but the emotion was void from the sound.

"You should probably go." She untangled her arms from him. "Trevor will come looking for me if I don't go back in."

"Be safe, please?" Erin's brown eyes melted right into her. It was never a matter of whether she could protect herself. He just wanted her to take precautions while doing so.

"Only if you will." She subconsciously wrapped her fingers around the ringed pendant. It offered a sense of closeness to him that she already felt slipping away, even though Erin still stood not two feet in front of her.

Erin's fingertips grazed her hand, lingering for a fraction of a moment before he left. His cloak accumulated the shadows of the alleys until he became one of them and was gone from sight. Their growing distance did nothing to ease the churning turmoil in her gut.

Chapter Twenty-Eight
An Eternity in a Day

Nothing in this place felt the same anymore. Her old room was exactly how she had left it. The scent in the air was unchanged, and it should have been all too easy to slip back into her old routine while she waited out the days.

It should have been, but something was different.

Maybe she was different.

When one day of waiting turned into three, Idalia found herself becoming increasingly more antsy. Any menial task that Trevor found for her to do never could capture her attention for long enough until she was distracted again. A worried daydreamer, that's what she was turning into.

"That's the fourth time you've looked at the door. I don't think they're going to magically spawn, Dilly."

"Can you not call me that anymore?" Idalia drummed her fingers on the table.

"But I thought it was our thing?"

Idalia looked at him. She didn't want to have a *thing* with Trevor. Perhaps if the circumstances had been vastly different, she wouldn't have minded so much. Now, the old nickname bogged her down. *It just wasn't the same as being referred to as a Jewel.*

"I'd prefer not to be called that." She rested her chin on the heel of her palm.

"Okay." Trevor shifted in his seat, "What do you say to some fresh air? Your lungs will thank you after spending so much time in that wasteland."

Idalia thought it might not be safe to admit that even her senses had acclimated to the slightly charred aroma of the Gate, so she simply nodded. They left the compound, and Trevor navigated them through the marketplaces and bustling atmosphere of the lower end of Thulta. One such market was positioned on an incline and when they reached it, Idalia found that she had a view of the Gate in all its perilous splendor. She had never thought that she could look upon it with a sense of longing. Idalia knew that it wasn't the Gate that she missed, but the Prince inside it.

"The horrors you must have seen there." Trevor sighed consolingly when he followed her line of sight.

"Come on, let me spoil you." He gave her a soft smile and held up a sky-blue shawl to her shoulders. "What do you think?"

"I... can't really see it." Idalia glanced behind her.

"Trust me, it's perfect for you."

"And where was that trust when-" She was about to say, '*when I needed you to listen,*' but a breeze carried a familiar scent to her nose that made her stop in her tracks.

Crackling firewood and spiced cider.

Was he here? That didn't make sense. Every logical bone in her body said to ignore it. However, her feet did not seem to approve of siding with common sense and carried her down the hill in the direction of that lovely smell, fast.

She finally stopped herself when she realized that the source of the scent was not coming from where she had hoped. Rather, it emanated from a rickety market stall and a large cast iron pot that a peddler was stirring.

"Idalia," Trevor gulped down air as he caught up to her.

"What in the world are you doing?"

I missed running." Came the curt reply.

Trevor rubbed a pressure point at the back of his neck.

"You could have gotten hurt."

Idalia steeled her gaze and turned to him. "Stop pretending that you actually care." She started back towards the compound, leaving Trevor to catch up behind her.

Idalia now had an overly enveloping sense of what true care was. Erin had given her that gift many times, in more ways than she could count.

It was a gift that would be difficult to repay, if she could manage to do so at all. How could she make the others see that Erin's crown was not discolored with the blood of the innocent, but merely tarnished with the type of stain that only guilt could leave? Idalia trained her gaze forward. She would fix this, somehow.

Or she would die trying.

Chapter Twenty-Nine
The Way You Hold Me

On the sixth day of her return to the compound, Trevor hounded her relentlessly to join him on his rounds. Idalia refused under the guise of a pain in her head. Truth be told, she was suffering from another type of ache entirely. She wondered how Erin was doing. Had he experienced another sleepwalking episode since she'd been gone? She made the decision to retire to her room just in case Trevor got the bright idea to come back for her. There was only one person that she wished to talk to, and they were separated by the largest waste of metal bordering Thulta.

Idalia figured that the best use of her time was to mentally memorize what she would say to the Sentries upon their return. The silent preparations drowned her senses, so she did not hear the first three knocks on her door. The fourth however...

"Trevor please, I told you. I'm not feeling well tonight." Idalia opened her door without as much as a second glance before she pressed her hand to his chest to push him back.

The visitor caught her hand. "Are you coming down with something, Jewel?"

Idalia whipped her head up, and the smallest hopeful noise escaped her throat at what she saw. While her visitor had donned a mask that was perfectly akin to Trevor's features, his eyes... Oh his eyes. They were unmistakable. Idalia pulled him into her room without warning and locked the door before throwing her arms around him. "I'm sorry, I know you said to leave but six days was all I could do." He murmured softly into her hair.

"I missed you." She whispered, "I really-"

"Me too." Erin affirmed, running a hand over the back of her head.

The way that the pair held on to each other, one almost might think that they'd been apart for months on end.

Perhaps time passes more slowly when you aren't with the one who makes your heart beat faster.

Eventually, they pulled apart. "You said you weren't feeling well, are you okay?" During their embrace, he'd allowed his mask to fall, and she looked upon the features which she had memorized.

"I'm physically fine." She offered with a slight raise to her shoulder.

"Well, that does leave other avenues open, Jewel. Emotionally, mentally, morally...the list goes on." He tilted his head, and Idalia found that the gesture warmed her heart.

"We'll have plenty of time to talk about that later, but right now I just want to hear about you." She squeezed his hands.

Erin hesitated for a moment but seeing as he clearly was not going to get her to budge, he replied, "You're going to think I'm joking, but when I went back without you, I swear on the stars that the castle was two shades darker."

Idalia chuckled, "You're right, I do think you're joking. Either that, or your night vision is fading."

Erin shook his head, "I've happened upon another reasoning but sure, we'll go with yours."

Idalia knew that this wasn't the time to ask reckless questions, but she'd spent the last several days in such a state of worry that some playful banter seemed rather appealing. "And what reasoning would that be?" A smile tugged at her lips as she plucked a loose thread from his cloak.

Erin was silent for a moment, and then she felt his hand graze past her ear. "This isn't you." He murmured to himself and brushed his fingers through her hair. In her peripheral vision she could tell that the dark color was fading back to her natural honeyed brunette.

"Your lips were perfect before." Erin took the pad of his thumb and lightly dragged it over her mouth, restoring the appearance of those as well. The delicate touch compelled Idalia's body to step closer to him.

"What are you doing?" Idalia whispered. Perhaps she was afraid that if she spoke too loudly, she would shatter this moment into pieces.

"Apologizing for changing what was already flawless."

His hand skimmed her shoulder and as Idalia glanced down at her hand, she saw her darker complexion reappear for the first time in months. Then his touch settled right where her neck met her jaw. "Are you sure you're okay? Your pulse is... kind of fast." Idalia had never heard such a combination of concern and hopefulness come from anyone. The fact that she heard it from his lips made the matter ten times more wonderful.

Idalia reached up and wrapped her fingers around his wrist. She could feel a steady thrumming of his pulse at first, but then she met his gaze and within milliseconds, the rhythm rapidly increased.

"Maybe we've come down with the same thing."

"Maybe I gave it to you." Erin's gentle gaze drank in her true features, almost as if he was trying to memorize the mapping of each one of her light freckles, before ultimately focusing on her eyes. "Idalia, I-"

A muffled clanging sound disrupted whatever his words would have been. *Voices. Lots of them.*

"They're back." Idalia's eyes widened as they darted from her door to the Prince and back again. "You have to get out of here." She whirled around to the window adjacent to them and shoved it open.

"Wait-" Erin dug his heels into the floor as Idalia tried to push him to the exit.

Idalia knew that if he lingered any longer, he could be at severe risk, but the traitorous part of her mind made her crave for him to finish whatever he was going to say before the ruckus.

He gave her a hurried smile and pressed his palm to her shoulder. Idalia felt warmth seep out from his fingertips and trail over her features. *He was changing her back with no regard to his own appearance.*

She felt a mixture of gratitude with a tinge of disappointment wash over her. Well, she could always ask him what he'd almost said another time.

Erin hoisted himself up and over the window ledge and dropped to the grass with a soft thud. Idalia stood on her toes to peer out into the night where he landed. "Don't forget to change yours." She whispered, as she gestured to his face.

"I'm not the one engaged to danger." Erin slid her an easy grin before he blended into the curling darkness.

Idalia's snicker was cut short by a booming knock on her door. When she opened it, she was immediately greeted by both Trevor and Mox.

"When you said she looked different I didn't think you meant-" Trevor silenced Mox by lightly jabbing his elbow into the other man's ribs.

"What? It's a good change." Mox threw his hands up in surrender, and Idalia bit back the urge to roll her eyes until after she'd pushed past them.

"Everyone is gathered, Dil... Idalia." Trevor jerked his chin towards one of the larger meeting rooms with one of the doors held slightly ajar.

When she entered the room, she immediately felt the heat of fourteen pairs of eyes on her back. She would not allow her cheeks to flame even when a scattered chorus of whistles filled the room.

"Who's this little temptress?" One Sentry's eyes roved over her when she stood at the front of the room.

"That's-" Trevor started, but she broke his sentence.

"Trevor." Idalia held her head higher. She was done with him answering for her. She didn't care if he thought he was being kind. She had gone through the Gate and back and survived. Not only that, but she had thrived with Erin.

"I'm still Idalia." Her voice rang clear, "Someone kind transformed me so that I would blend in."

"Someone kind?" Another Sentry snickered. "In that place? I doubt it. Freaks and demons, the lot of them."

Her mind snapped to Erin's gentle gaze and featherlight voice, and she fought the desire to glare on his behalf.

"Why did you go to Esterod?" She placed her palms flat on the table and shifted her gaze to Mox.

"We rounded up reinforcements, we're going to strike before they can turn their wrath on us."

Idalia's throat went dry. "What? I thought this entire plot was to keep the bloodshed to a minimum."

Mox's eyebrows flicked up. "It's either their blood or ours."

"You have to call them off." Idalia blurted, "There's no cause for war."

The Sentry that had previously remarked on her appearance leant back in his chair and folded his hands behind his bald head. "It's been a long time coming, girl. Don't be so naïve as to think that they'd ever outright tell you about a war." He gave her a pointed look that repulsed her to her core.

"Which one of us has lived there for months and actually interacted with these people you call demons?" Idalia's voice dropped like plummeting daggers into fire.

The man's eyebrows narrowed as he sat up to retort, but Trevor cleared his throat.

"They're right, Idalia." He cast his line of sight to the floor. "The Thultan's are practically defenseless without us. If we don't eradicate those across the Gate now, everything could be lost."

"Not all of them are evil." Idalia clenched her fist behind her back. She took three silent deep inhales to calm the sparking nerves in her body. "When do we attack?"

Mox opened and closed his mouth and shared a look with Trevor. "Soon." Was all he said.

"If we're done here," the other Sentry yawned and stood to his feet, several joints popping in the process, "we should hit the hay." With that said, several other Sentries trailed behind him out the door, and the train continued until she was left in the echoing space with Trevor. Idalia felt numb. *What had she done?*

"Please tell them not to do this." She whispered. Idalia never begged, and the thought of doing so to Trevor made her stomach turn. For Erin, though... she would get on her knees and plead until her throat bled.

"It will be better this way." Trevor clasped his hands behind his back.

"If you do this, you're no better than the villains on the other side." She gritted her teeth.

Trevor exhaled slowly. "Get some rest, we'll find a new station assignment for you in the morning. Your work across the Gate is done."

Trevor left without knowing that a decision had already been cemented in Idalia's mind. She wouldn't be here in the morning. She was going back to the Gate, to Erin.

Idalia pulled herself up to her window sill, much like how Erin had done just mere hours before. The knowledge of this impending doom felt like a storm looming on the horizon with its dark clouds and deafening thunder. She knew that there was no way to stop this storm, but she could brace for it.

Chapter Thirty
Undeserving of That Mercy

Brambles and thorned vines dug into her skin as she raced back to the Gate. Idalia didn't feel the sting, the sensations were overpowered by her faltering determination that this could still be fixed. Erin had promised that he'd leave an entrance open for her, and she doubted it would be in the front. By the Author, this blasted Gate seemed to be stretching out on its own, presenting the illusion that it spanned indefinitely.

Finally, *finally*. She found that space where the metal curves parted just enough for her to slip in. Her shirt got caught and the sleeve ripped where the seam met her shoulder. In her haste to jerk her arm free, the Gate clanged against itself. If it hadn't been so deathly quiet, the noise would have gone unnoticed. To her dismay, a guard stepped around the corner that very instant and locked eyes with her.

Erin, where are you? She tried to reverse her steps. If she could crawl back to the other side-

Then he was upon her.

A scream built in her throat but the hand that covered her mouth stifled it. She clawed at his arm and hand, fighting to get away.

He hissed when her nails drew blood from the deep scratches on his skin. "Quit it." His gruff voice scratched her ears.

"Let go of me." Idalia whipped her head free from his hand.

The racket that they were making attracted the attention of yet another guard on his rounds and Idalia felt her shred of hope shatter. "What did you wrangle up, Thompson?"

The guard that held Idalia wrenched her arms behind her back, and a grunt of pain left her. "Some idiot girl." He growled.

"Please I have to see-" She tried to speak but the man pulled her arms back even further, and Idalia felt a muscle nearly tear.

"She's crazed. I'll throw her down there before the rotation shifts." The other guard took another step closer to them, and Idalia's arms were gratefully released. However, she wasn't sure how thankful she should be since she was only being transferred into the hands of a different guard.

Her new captor led her away and into the palace. "I need to speak with the Prince." Idalia tried to cement her feet into the marble floor, but that was a nearly impossible task with how smooth the surface was. Her boots would have slid from underneath her if she continued.

"I'm taking you to him."

She felt a glimmer of hope flare in her heart before it was doused with the thick smog of wary doubt. "Which one?"

"You ask a lot of questions." The new guard readjusted his hold on her arm, and while it wasn't tight enough to leave dark bruises, her hand felt cold from the hindered blood flow.

Relief crashed over her in a wave when the guard rapped on Erin's door.

"Enter." His voice floated to their ears from the inside. The guard clicked the door open, and all but hurled Idalia at Erin's feet.

The Prince's caramel eyes went wide in alarm at her wince and dismissed the guard with the wave of his wrist.

"Jewel, are you hurt?" He knelt to the floor in front of her.

All the words that Idalia wanted to say, *needed* to say, fled from her voice like startled birds. When she locked eyes with him, all she could see were the horrific images that her mind conjured. She imagined the Sentries breaking through the Gate, trampling the iron like blades of grass. She pictured the grave image of everyone below in the dungeon bleeding and begging for mercy before Erin could have offered them the chance for a better life.

Erin. Would she be forced to watch as Mox drove a sword between his ribs? She couldn't bear having to live with the weight of knowing that all he worked to protect had slipped from his fingers... because of her.

Idalia couldn't answer him because she *was* hurt. Hurt that the people who she had seen as her friends and family disregarded the only thing that she had ever asked of them. However, that pain didn't compare to the guilt that she felt gnawing at her very insides because Erin was holding her. He should be angry and turn her away for having a hand in wrecking his life. But here he was, coaxing her breathing to slow as her tears dampened his jacket. Then she realized that he didn't know about the attack yet, and it was selfish of her to wish that he never would. It pained her, but she shrugged out of his tender hold and got to her feet.

"Idalia." His tone was heavy with concern, and his hand hovered in the air between them. In her muddled mind, she wasn't sure if he was trying to reach for her or keep her at arm's length.

"Erin- I…" The words choked her.

"Did they hurt you?"

"I messed up, I messed up." She buried her head in her hands.

"No, it's going to be alright, just breathe."

"I thought I was doing the right thing-"

"You did what you thought was right, that's all anyone could ask of you." He took a step towards her, but Idalia pressed her palm flat against his chest to keep him from advancing further. Then her hand slipped as a soft sob left her.

"I just… wanted to be their equal."

He caught her hand and pressed the gentlest of kisses to her inner wrist, "My darling, Queens don't concern themselves with fools."

Idalia's breath caught, and she hung her head to avoid his eyes. "I'm no queen, I'm a wretched traitor. You gave me your friendship and your trust, and I didn't stop this when I should have."

"Don't say that." Erin murmured. Before he could get another word out, her own poured out in a rush. "They're going to attack the castle."

"The Sentries?"

"Yes. They've secured an alliance with Esterod soldiers." Idalia swallowed, and her throat felt as if it was crafted from sandpaper.

"Okay."

One word. That was all. No reprimand or look of disgust and hate. Somehow, that felt worse than the alternative.

"How are you okay with this?" Idalia blurted. "I messed up so badly, and you act as if you're fine with everything?"

Erin watched her calmly, "Do you think I'm going to fault you for doing what you thought was right?"

"I wish you would." She bit out, "I wish you would stop dragging this out because I am terrified-" Her voice dropped to a whisper. "I am *terrified* that I'll wake up and you'll hate me, and I'd rather get that heartbreak out of the way." Idalia's chest heaved, as if her ribcage wasn't enough to contain these violently swirling emotions.

Erin's lips pursed into a thin line, and she braced herself as she watched her words pierce through the growing silence.

He didn't falter, his countenance never changed. It wasn't until the room started to blur that she felt his arms envelop her. "It's okay, I mean it." Erin whispered, and she clung to his chest. Clung to the man whom everyone feared, who was her safety.

"Please forgive me." Idalia wasn't sure if the words had sound or if she only mouthed them. "I've been on the wrong side."

"I know you've felt like everything was somehow your fault, like you could have changed something if only you'd have made a different choice."

A broken noise left her, and Idalia tightened her hold on his shirt. Idalia had spent so long navigating an inconsistent path with no one to lean on to give her balance. But Erin was firm, he was steady. An anchored presence amongst uneven ground.

"I need you to know-" He pulled back from her and tilted her tear-streaked chin towards his face. "Even if everything falls apart, I would have wanted to know you, I would have wanted to be with you."

She swallowed; her throat felt so tight that she was certain the words couldn't be choked out.

"I've only made everything worse."

Erin pressed a kiss to her forehead, and the warmth of his lips spread through her trembling body, offering a sense of reprieve.

"We'll figure it out." Erin took a deep breath, and she felt his chest rise and fall against her. "This war was inevitable, something would have triggered it eventually. Don't be too harsh on yourself, Jewel."

"What do we do? They wouldn't listen. They aren't going to call it off." Idalia shut her eyes and rested her forehead against his inner shoulder.

Erin was silent for a long moment before he spoke again. "We fight."

The Murmur

There's something so utterly horrible about feeling hopeless. It puts a damper on everything that a person sees and does, because they can't help but expect the worst. I have seen many cases of such hopelessness, but in her tears, I saw years of pain and questions that had no remedy. I am no stranger to that ache. There are days even now, that I feel it.

Chapter Thirty-One
The Light in the Void

That night, Idalia was pulled from her fitful sleep by the sound of rustling pages. The room was dark behind her eyelids, save for a warm flickering glow to her left. She pried her eyes open to find the source, only to see Erin poring over a stack of heavy books at his table. He'd forgone his jacket, which was probably carelessly crumpled somewhere on the floor and used one hand to flip through the pages while the other rubbed circles behind his neck.

"Why are you awake?" Idalia yawned, and Erin's gaze snapped up like a bolt of lightning. She squinted in the darkness to the clock on his wall. It was well into the night.

"Just studying. You can go back to sleep." He offered her a gentle smile, but it did nothing to mask the flicker of worry that she could have sworn she caught in his gaze.

"There's no use in being up by yourself." Idalia stretched her arms over her head and winced at that sore muscle.

"There's also no use in staying up for no reason, sweet one." Erin's fingers paused over a block of text to focus on her.

Idalia ducked her face so that the candlelight wouldn't catch the scarlet color that crept up her cheeks. "If you're trying to flatter me into listening, it won't work."

"I figured as much." Erin shook his head and angled his head back over the book.

"Can I help?" Idalia strode over to the desk and ran her fingertips along the spine of one particularly substantial book.

"Hmm, actually can you hand me that?" He dipped his chin towards the book she touched, and she offered it to him.

"What are these monstrosities?" She peeked over his slouched shoulder.

"Our laws." Was the mumbled reply as he inched the candelabra closer. *How tired was he that he was struggling to see in this light?*

"Are you looking for something specific?" She hopped up on the side of the desk and hauled a new book into her lap before flipping through its pages. Along its spine was the title, *The Regulations of Rayavin.*

"See if you can find something on the marital plead."

Idalia quirked a brow, "That brings me to my next question. What's that?"

Erin shifted a page in between his forefinger and thumb. "Regardless of how twisted this system is, a prisoner has the chance to be spared from death if their spouse pleads for them. To be honest with you, I think Lester only allows it because he enjoys watching others grovel."

"Is someone in the dungeon in need of it?" Idalia asked as she scanned the text. *For a place so unlawful, there were an abhorrent number of both spoken and unspoken rules.* "Don't you have the power to plead for them?"

"I hope we won't have to use it." Erin replied more quietly before adding, "I have complete confidence that Lester would never accept a plead from me. He would refuse just to dangle his power over my head and then no one is safe." Idalia noticed that he was propping his head up with a tired hand before his eyes tracked to the clock. "Wake me up in fifteen minutes, please?"

"Forty-five." She countered.

"Thirty." Erin gave her a small chuckle and folded his arms atop the law texts before burying his head in them.

She heard his breathing deepen within the first ten minutes. *When was the last time he had slept?*

Idalia read through chapters upon chapters of regulations and commands. There were several regarding fair trials that Lester had obviously overlooked, but Idalia figured that he wouldn't care even if he was aware of their existence.

This book alone was a guideline of a more peaceful way to rule this place. It wasn't the laws that were instilling fear into everyone, but rather the Prince that dominated the throne. Idalia raised her eyes from the paragraph to the sleeping boy in front of her. According to this, a Prince of the Gate could only become King on his twenty-fifth birthday. Since Lester was the firstborn... the thought made Idalia shiver.

Erin was the one who deserved to rule. He would make a wonderful King, if only given the chance. In her mind's eye, she envisioned a future after this horrible war was over. If Lester was gone, there would be nothing to hold Erin back from reigning and fixing everything that his brother had tried to destroy. It hurt a little too much to also imagine what would become of them together if he were to take on the mantle of King. Erin would need a wise Queen beside him one day, not a clumsy traitor who couldn't be trusted with her own heart.

Oh, but despite all this, she wished on whatever glimmer of magic that still lingered in this world, for her secret dream to remain with him to come true.

Because although she felt undeserving, in that moment it felt within her reach. They were simply a broken girl, and a burdened Prince with hearts that reached for the other like two stars spanning the night sky.

Idalia had never put much stock in fate, but if there was ever a time to beseech for its strings to become untangled, it was now.

Chapter Thirty-Two
More Than Art

The sunlight crept through the parted billowing drapes, highlighting the next category of laws that Idalia rummaged through. She had learned so much in just several hours, and each turn of the page invigorated her.

"Liar." A soft voice met her ears and Idalia jolted from her concentration. Erin blinked at her sleepily, although his eyes no longer held the exhaustion that she had seen several hours ago.

"What?"

"You said you'd wake me up in thirty minutes."

Idalia gave him her best innocent grin, although the glint in her eyes made her look slyer than an angel. "I got wrapped up in these." She waved a hand to the stack of texts that had accumulated as the night wore on. "Besides, you're cute when you're tired." She added under her breath.

Erin raised his head and propped his chin up on his arm.

"You think I'm cute?" There was a hint of boyish mischief in his voice, as if he was testing the waters of what he could get away with so early in the morning. Idalia knew what he was trying to do, so she schooled her features into neutrality and casually flicked her gaze back to her book.

"Only when you're asleep."

Erin chuckled and straightened, his back was surely sore from sleeping hunched over, but he didn't reveal any signs of discomfort. "My feelings. I'm wounded." He made a show of draping a ringed hand over his heart, and Idalia held back her smile. "I never said you weren't *handsome* all the other hours of the day." She mumbled, and quickly darted her eyes down to the book.

Idalia heard Erin smile and then he tipped her book lower with his finger. "What have you figured out?"

"Well... it's a lot, and quite honestly this place would be astoundingly less fearsome if your lovely brother would actually read these laws."

Erin murmured his agreement, "Oh, he's aware of them. They were drilled into our heads as children but Lester rules as if they are nonexistent."

"I just-" Idalia hopped off of the table, "How come he's the one that calls the shots? You're the more powerful one, and yet-" She furrowed her brow.

"Yet he's made me his twisted lackey?" Erin finished for her, and she confirmed with a nod.

"Father saw the same weakness in me, that he saw in my mother. Truthfully, I think he blamed her for it, but she gave him a firstborn that was his spitting image and that settled things in his mind. He set it in stone that Lester would ascend the throne first, and that left me not much room for argument." Erin dragged his hands through his hair. "It took me too long to realize that the "weakness" he found in her and I was not a curse, but a strength."

Idalia angled her body to slightly lean forward against the desk, as if supported by the will to soak in each of his words. "So, I know the things that I fix, and try to heal will never erase what I've done but-" Erin peered down at his hands, as a shaft of sunlight shifted over the skin. "I wanted the only thing that relates me to Lester to be our shared blood. Not the culmination of our actions." A half laugh left his lips, "And frankly I'd rather not be related, but there's no way around that one."

Idalia knew what she was about to say was wishful thinking, but she had a feeling that soon, there wouldn't be any more time for wishes. "What would you do, if you were king?"

Erin leaned back in his chair, studying her. "Abolish these torture and death sentences for one. This is the only home I've ever known, and I'd want for people to think of it without a torrent of fear." He cocked his head, "I would help more people. Even those that have accepted another chance aren't a drop in the bucket compared to the multitude who have died here without one." Erin's eyes held such a heaviness in them. It was like watching something sink to the bottom of the sea with no hope of breaking through the surface again. That weight seemed to ease when Idalia settled her hand atop his own. "What would you do?" He asked suddenly.

Idalia watched him quizzically and then made a show of looking over herself, "Clearly, I can't be a king, so my answer is futile." A playful smile danced on her lips.

Erin shook his head, "Humor me."

She took a deep breath through her nose and thought about it. "Well on the surface I'd make this place look brighter." Idalia scanned her surroundings. Erin's room was the most non-ominous space that she had seen in this castle, and that was saying something. "Maybe paint the Gate white and clear out all the dead plants and trees. We could take inspiration from Sylvie's Oasis." Idalia's smile was dazzling as excitement bled into her words, and Erin squeezed her hand with a sweet pressure, encouraging her to go on. "My main focus would be to bring light to the Gate. Some much-needed light."

"I would love that." Erin rubbed his thumb in circles along her hand. "And if we're speaking of things we would change, I'd never put my magic on you again. Although it never masked the most beautiful thing about you." His other hand reached up to tap the space under her collarbone. *Her heart.*

Idalia held her breath, which did nothing to slow her heartbeat as it tripped over itself like an uncoordinated dancer. "You're the only one that doesn't prefer this look better than what I really am." She shook her head.

Erin tipped her chin back up just enough to look into her eyes. "Seems like we both savor what's under the surface instead of the façade."

Oh, Author. His gentle voice and the completely unguarded look in his eyes was more alluring than the promise of a thousand castles, or unimaginable wealth. She was finding that each word from his lips was like a treasure, in the sense that sometimes there were buried, hidden meanings within them that she craved to uncover.

For a moment, the only thing that mattered was his hand on hers, and the hopeful tension in the air that begged her to take a step closer to the Prince. For a lingering second, all of their wishful thinking felt as if it could cement into place and become a new reality. *Their* reality. When Idalia took that bold step closer, her hip brushed against a book that teetered precariously close to the edge, and the slight jostle caused it to plummet to the floor in between their feet with a loud *smack*.

She imagined that the delicate moment which they had forged also fell from the side and shattered along with the book and its many splayed pages.

"Oh-" Idalia quickly knelt down to retrieve it. As she plucked it from the ground, a small rectangular piece of paper freed itself from its previously wedged position and fluttered down in a spiral. Idalia handed Erin the book and swept up the little square.

"I wonder what that is?" He noted the change in color and texture from this piece of paper to the book it had fallen from. Idalia shrugged a shoulder and unfolded it.

It wasn't a note, or even a stray bookmark. The object in question was a picture, and judging by the black graphite smudges that came away on Idalia's fingertips, it was a pencil sketched portrait. The subject of the art was a beautiful young woman with long dark hair wreathed in wildflowers that flowed to her belted waist. She leant against a wall with her head angled towards the artist. The picture was done so realistically, that Idalia felt as if she could reach into the art and touch the other girl.

"I know her." Idalia murmured. A sense of familiarity and reminiscence pulled at her core. Erin stood from his chair and peered over Idalia's shoulder, and she heard him draw in a quick breath.

"This is the woman that found me when I ran away. My white flower lady." Idalia smiled and made sure that he had a clear view of the image. "Why in the world was she in that law book?" Idalia furrowed her brow and glanced at the forgotten volume. She gingerly turned the slip of paper over to check for an inscription. Then she found one.

Sylvie Amias.

Idalia felt her thoughts simultaneously stop and blur around her. "She's-"

"My mother." Erin spoke from behind her with the same tenderness in his tone that she remembered hearing whenever he mentioned her.

Idalia set the photo down carefully, as if she was scared that placing it too harshly would cause that beautiful moment in time to disintegrate before she turned to face him.

"So, I *did* get to meet her." There was a somber sweetness in her voice, mirroring what she felt in her heart. Erin's eyes lingered on the photo, as if he could etch it into his mind to have one more moment with the woman who had loved him so. Then he did something that Idalia had not been expecting and gathered her into his arms.

"She told me about you." Erin said softly into her hair, and Idalia found herself melting into his embrace without a second thought. As if it were her second nature. Then she realized what he'd uttered. *I found her mama; I found the one you told me about.* His subconscious words in the dark that night rang clearly through her mind, and she tightened her hold on him. "How did you know it was me?"

A soft chuckle reverberated through his chest, "She told me to watch out for you." Erin pulled away enough for her to see him. "She said there was a young girl with brown eyes like mine, and a fire in her that was unmistakable. She said you would need someone to stoke those embers, not extinguish them."

Idalia felt her eyes begin to mist over. How was it that a woman whom she had met once, could have left such a lasting impact on her?

"She said that the girl had these freckles on her cheekbones that looked like constellations." Erin's fingertips traced over Idalia's cheek, as if remembering every detail of her hidden complexion. "I had no doubt that you were the one when we met."

Idalia leaned into his touch, "So that's why you saved me."

A flash of memory pertaining to that night swirled in her mind when he showed her his reformation program and she had uttered those very words.

"That's why you saved me too..."

"That wasn't the only reason, Jewel, but I think I've given you enough of an information overload for one night."

Erin chuckled again in the present, "Yes. I trusted her intuition then, and-" He drew in a breath and looked into her eyes. "It was the best choice I could have made."

Idalia had always heard people assimilate *that* feeling to butterflies fluttering about in one's stomach. However, when he looked at her, the sensation was not akin to butterflies. Rather, she could only describe it as the thunderous beating of the wings of great birds as they soared from her heart to fill the rapidly closing gap between them.

He inclined his head down, while she tilted her chin up. Their lips brushed with the gentleness of a pleading whisper. Careful, promising, longing. Perhaps if one of them had lingered, the other would have given in more fully.

Sometimes, a breath of love speaks louder than every shouted declaration.

The Murmur

I made a decision that day. It didn't matter if this castle fell into rubble around us, or if we had to start anew. I would protect her with my very last breath. I would be the one to keep that fire within her ignited, never to fizzle out.

If only I had known that she would be the one to protect me.

Chapter Thirty-Three
Silent Promise

The issue with dreams is that they are short-lived. They can transport a person to a wonderful place filled with decadent moments and heartwarming words. However, reality comes to splinter away that heaven until all that is left are the fragments of a memory. Idalia felt that their tender moment was like that. Something beautiful, wreathed in peace and for a moment, all of their worries had dissipated like smoke. But smoke follows fire, and fire means destruction.

That fate was exactly what every borrowed second ticked toward if they didn't fix this. The next couple of days fell into a similar routine. Erin would disappear to carry out whatever tasks Lester forced upon him during the day while Idalia practically ransacked the multitude of law texts in search of answers to a list that Erin had given her. She caught a darting flicker of pain in his eyes when he read through her notes on that marital plead, but she wasn't quite sure why. If anything, wouldn't that plead give a prisoner a better chance of living? Perhaps it bothered him that he couldn't be the one to petition on a prisoner's behalf.

Idalia was not allowed the luxury of thinking about it for long, for there was much to do, too little time, and she needed to meet Erin. During the cover of nightfall, they both would slip down into the prison and try to convince as many captives as possible to accept a second chance. Lester's awful methods of psychological and physical torture had left many prisoners in such a state of fear that they were terrified to leave.

Erin had been running non-stop with barely a wink of sleep. However, his outward appearance betrayed his exhaustion. He looked as unruffled as ever, which Idalia admired except she had a sinking suspicion that his composure was as much for her benefit as it was for his. She watched him make a mental calculation of the number of prisoners in the cells and then he nodded his head to the left. "I'll go left, can you take the right?"

"Of course." They didn't have the privilege of communicating with the prisoners together, so they had been splitting up in order to reach as many as possible in a night.

It wouldn't be long before they would need to sneak the willing ones out under the cover of darkness, before the Sentries attacked. Idalia wasn't sure when she had stopped thinking of herself as one of them. It turned out, she belonged in the very place that she had spent her whole life fearing. Her gut twisted; *she had figured that out too late.*

Chains dragged across stone as she walked by the iron doors and the hair that raised on her arms signaled that someone was watching her. She looked at their sunken cheeks and bony frames. How many of them were here just because they needed to eat and had to steal so that they and their families could live? She started at one end of the hallway and talked to each prisoner individually. Then her eyes landed on a huddled silhouette in the corner of the last cell that watched Idalia with a look of wariness. Idalia recognized that one, it was the woman who had practically dragged her assumption of Erin's character through the mud. There was such hate there. Upon closer inspection, perhaps there was a facet of pain behind the venom that she spewed.

"Hi." Idalia said softly and sat down in front of her cell. The woman shifted and looked Idalia up and down in distaste before she opened her mouth to croak out a response. It took a moment, as if she hadn't used her words since that burst of fury during their first interaction.

"Never seen an executioner in a dress." The woman's voice sounded like sandpaper against splintering wood.

Idalia glanced down at the wine-colored, crushed velvet dress that she wore, so at odds with the dirt and grime of this place. "I'm not here to kill you." Idalia swallowed.

The older woman huffed. "Then tell whoever will, to be quick about it. I'm tired of waiting."

Idalia's shoulders drooped at the words. "You can't mean that."

A bitter chuckle escaped the woman, "Why not? What's there to live for?" She waved a chained wrist towards the depressing surroundings.

"Life itself." Idalia inched closer to the cell, "What if I told you that you could get out of here?"

Idalia had expected some spark of hope, or curiosity to flare in her eyes, but the woman's gaze was as dull and closed-off as ever.

"Don't you want to try to live?"

The woman closed her eyes and leant back against the stone wall, not saying anything more. Idalia was about to push herself to her feet when the woman rasped, "He's gone."

"Who is?"

"My Thomas." She whispered, and the flickering torch-light on the adjacent wall highlighted a single tear that rolled down the leathery texture of her skin. "He was all I had."

Idalia slipped her hand through the sharp curve in the door. It stung, but something in her begged to give this woman a bit of comfort. Perhaps it was because one broken heart can easily sympathize with another. "I'm sorry." She murmured.

The woman swallowed thickly, "If I die, I can see him again."

"Did he love you?" Idalia asked suddenly.

A grief-stricken smile twitched on the woman's lips for half of a second. "Yes."

"I never met your Thomas," Idalia uttered quietly. "But I know that when you love someone, you would never want them to be miserable."

"It wouldn't be fair," The woman's voice quivered. "For me to live when he didn't get to."

"It can feel like that sometimes, but isn't it better to live and honor his memory than to let your grief swallow you?"

The woman cast a pointed glance at her. "What do you know about love?"

"Honestly?" Idalia took a breath, "Not much." Then her fingers wrapped around the cool metal of the golden band around her neck. "But I'm learning."

"If something happened to you, would you be okay with your love moving on as if nothing happened?" The woman rotated her body at an angle facing Idalia.

Idalia traced over the ringed pendant until the grooves indented on her thumb. Erin's features immediately materialized in her mind's eye. "I'd be thankful for what time we did have, but I would want him to be happy."

The woman swallowed again, "I don't know how to be happy without him, not anymore."

"Maybe-" Idalia started, "Maybe the first step is to take one day at a time. Until you are able to find happiness in other things, you have the memories to give you peace."

"You don't think it'd be betraying him?" She asked in such a small voice, that it was hard to believe it came from such a gruff woman. Perhaps that's what grief does to a person. It causes layers of a shell to form around the heart because deep down, the person knows that if the armor cracks, it would reveal the shattered heart within.

"I think you should live *for* him." Idalia's words came out in a whisper, and the other woman's eyes turned watery.

"But how?" She asked, holding up her wrists whose chains clattered against themselves.

"We have a plan, but you have to trust both of us." Idalia's eyes flicked to the left corridor just as Erin's footsteps neared them.

The vulnerability that the prisoner had let Idalia see quickly shuttered when Erin came into view, and her posture went rigid. "Trust *him*?" Her words were grating.

"Getting you out of here was his idea." Idalia tried to assure her, but the woman's gaze held a burning amount of suspicion.

"Trust goes both ways, sweet one." Erin murmured to Idalia and slid a key into the cell lock where it echoed with a resounding *click*. Idalia watched as Erin stepped inside the cell near the woman. He knelt in front of her before using a different, smaller key to unlock the shackles that bound her to the floor.

"Why are you doing this?" The woman's raspy voice crackled as she rubbed the sore skin on her wrists. "Aren't you a monster?"

If that comment stung him, it didn't show. "I'm trying to right the wrongs of my family." He replied and helped the woman to her feet. With her hands free, she could have turned on him and tried to strangle the life from his throat, but she didn't.

Trust goes both ways.

"Be ready for tomorrow. We'll take you along with the others to a safe place, but under no circumstances can you ever come back here." Erin told her.

A sound that resembled both a scoff and a laugh left the woman. "I have no desire to think about the likes of this place ever again." Then her focus switched to Idalia, "I'll think about you though." Her chapped lips twitched with what Idalia knew was a semblance of a smile. The woman swiped away the tracks of tears on her cheeks before she faced Erin.

"You be good to that girl, I'm still not sure you deserve her."

Erin chuckled gently, "I don't." He replied as he stepped back out with Idalia and closed the door, ensuring the guards would not be suspicious during their next rotations.

As they began the trek up the stairs, Idalia stole a glance of Erin's profile when she thought he wasn't looking. It didn't help that she had mistimed her glimpse because he'd tried to steal one of his own at that very same moment.

"I thought that last woman would be the hardest to convince, how did you do it?" He asked thoughtfully.

Idalia toyed with her necklace, "I tried to speak to her heart, not her head. She just needed hope."

Erin draped his arm around her shoulders and pulled her closer as they ascended the steps. "Thank you."

Idalia could have drowned in the comforting warmth seeping from him and into her, but she knew that if she inched any closer, they both would trip.

"You don't actually feel that way, do you?" She asked after a moment.

"Feel what way?" Erin paused before the next landing to turn his attention to her.

"Like you don't deserve me."

Erin smiled, "I don't, but I'll never stop trying to be deserving of you, no matter how long it takes."

Idalia reached to cup his cheek in her hand, "Tell me that there's a future for us, Erin. Because I would wait an eternity for it. For you." She admitted, and an awed breath left him.

"It's not going to be easy." He swallowed and stroked her cheek with his fingertips.

"Nothing good ever is." She murmured, lashes fluttering against his hand.

Erin rested his forehead against hers, and an unspoken message passed between them. They weren't just fighting to save everyone else. They were fighting to save their own future. This moment was a silent promise that turned the ties that connected their hearts from strings to bonds of steel.

Perhaps not all dreams have to shatter.

Chapter Thirty-Four
The Passage

There were a number of tasks that needed to be considered before they could transfer the first wave of captives to their sanctuary. The timing, the guard rotation, the number of souls that could go with them at a time, and the weather of all things contributed. Dark clouds had been slowly encroaching upon the sky for the past several hours, threatening to unleash a torrent of blinding sheets of rain on their heads at any moment.

Unfortunately, Erin and Idalia did not have the luxury of waiting the storm out. A water-drenched cloak was the much better alternative to one soaked in blood. Everyone could hear the rumbling thunder from this pit of a dungeon.

Idalia carried a stack of guard uniforms in her arms, as Erin went down the line to change the features of a few more notorious faces. He had already shifted ten prisoners, all while keeping a tight tether on Idalia's appearance.

She wasn't quite sure how he was managing the strain on his magic, but he never complained once. The only signals that this process was draining his energy were a slight twitch in his jaw and he flexed and unflexed his hands behind his back like one would do with a muscle cramp.

"Those of you that I've altered, go to Idalia." Erin waved a hand in her direction and Idalia passed out a set of uniforms to every male in line before they dispersed back to their cells to change. Having some of the prisoners pose as Gate guards was their backup plan if something went terribly wrong. They would have to think on their feet if they were caught, and Idalia prayed that all of the captives in this group were good actors. The last man in Idalia's makeshift line fell silent when she handed him the ensemble.

"Are you alright?" She asked.

Tears welled up in the prisoner's eyes, "I just can't believe I'll get to see my daughter again." He dipped his chin in thanks and scurried off to his cell. The rest of the prisoners chattered quietly amongst themselves, although several stayed deathly quiet.

Idalia subtly brushed Erin's hand with her own, and she felt his hand tremble. Erin glanced down at her, reading the unspoken question in her eyes. "I'm fine, sweet one."

"Is there a way I can learn how to do your magic in the next thirty minutes so I can help?" She tilted her head.

Erin chuckled, "I'm not so sure that it can be taught, but I appreciate it." His thumb tenderly traced the curve of her chin for a brief second before one of the prisoners began to ask him questions.

Perhaps it was just as well that a prisoner needed help at that moment because Idalia needed to focus, and it was much too easy to become distracted by the warmth in his eyes. *One day*. She told herself. *One day when this is all over, I will welcome every distraction that he brings.*

Half an hour later, the men had changed, and the women had donned coal black, hooded cloaks to better blend in with the shadows of night.

"I'm going to go over this once more, just to be sure that everyone understands what is about to happen." Erin stood at the foot of the staircase. "There's twenty-three of you, which means that we're breaking into two groups. The first group, will go ahead with me and the second group will follow closely behind with Idalia."

Erin waited to make sure everyone had muttered an agreement before continuing, "We cannot, under any circumstances, draw unnecessary attention to ourselves. Be as quiet as possible, or we're all dead."

That elicited a few snickers from the prisoners, but Idalia had a gut feeling that Erin had not meant for that comment to be lighthearted. With that, Erin tugged his own hood over his hair but not before ensuring that Idalia's was in place. She took advantage of their closeness by murmuring, "You be careful, okay?"

Erin gave her a smile that sent shivers through her, "I don't do anything halfway, darling." Then his shoulders slumped a bit as he let his guard down for Idalia. "Be careful too."

"You don't want me to be engaged to danger anymore?" She chuckled.

"Not before I have a chance." He said under his breath, and it nearly knocked the air out of her lungs as his words sunk in. Idalia didn't have the opportunity to respond before several prisoners prodded them forward, all eager to be free of this dungeon. Idalia lingered behind the first group as they climbed the stairs before the rest followed.

They traded the stale air of the dungeon for the whipping winds of the outside, and it was a fight to simply keep the hood from flying back from Idalia's face. Strikes of lightning cracked the sky into pieces, reminiscent of a shattered mirror with raindrops falling like shards of glass. Moments like this taught Idalia to be even more grateful for the little blessings. Thankful, for the rattling creak of the Gate as it clanged against the fierce air currents which drowned out the crunch of their many footsteps. Erin helped each prisoner one by one through the gap in the Gate until every man and woman took their first strides into the freedom that they never thought they would taste again.

The sky opened its floodgates and pelted them with rain as the groups fled with Erin as their leader. Several older prisoners stumbled behind as the squelching mud came to claim their feet, and Idalia helped to pry them loose. Idalia felt a distinct stinging sensation lash across her wrist, but she put that aside. The storm was turning their path into a mudslide, though not one prisoner uttered a complaint.

Compared to what they had already faced, jagged rocks and wet, churned earth were nothing. They couldn't risk bringing along any lanterns, so the first group was relying on Erin's uncanny ability to see through the pitch-black night. Idalia's charges had to depend on grabbing the sleeves of those in front of them and the rapid flashes of lightning that offered split seconds of illumination for their next steps.

Erin led them into Thulta through the many twisting alleyways and back roads. Idalia did not even recognize them from the countless rounds she had completed as a Sentry. Perhaps that was an incredibly beneficial thing. If she couldn't recall this path, then she was certain that none of the other Sentries were aware of its existence. Idalia kept glancing over her shoulder to make sure that no one was left behind or strayed from the group.

Finally, they made it to the refuge. A mumbled chorus of questions flowed through the two groups that had now joined to form a small crowd. Erin rapped on the door and even from Idalia's position in the back, she could clearly see Mama Rose's features. The older woman's face was lit with the warm glow of the house behind her. Her eyes widened in surprise as she looked upon all the unexpected guests.

Erin said something to her, and Idalia watched Mama Rose nod her chin twice before ushering everyone aside. Idalia was the last one to cross the threshold, and as she shut the door behind her, she heard Mama Rose say, "How many more?"

"Twenty." Erin peeled the soaked cloak from his shoulders, "Some of them aren't ready yet, but we're running out of time."

Mama Rose nodded again, "It will be cramped, but we will make it work. Some of us can sleep outside if we have to." Erin rested a hand on her shoulder, "Thank you."

She gave him that motherly smile and then her gaze landed on Idalia, "Glad to see you stuck around, child."

Idalia walked over to stand by Erin's side. "There's nowhere I'd rather be."

Mama Rose gave her a thoughtful look and then replied,

"Take that cloak off before you catch even more of a chill."

Idalia chuckled and pried the fabric from where it clung to her. She was soaked to the bone and realized that her clothes were dripping rainwater to form a puddle where she stood. Idalia folded her cloak over her arm and glanced at Erin, who wore a worried expression.

"What is it?"

"Rose, can you bring me a bandage?" Erin asked before he gathered Idalia's left hand into his own. The light reflected off of the trickle of blood that ran down her hand. "How badly does it hurt?" He looked at her before he unrolled the bandage.

Idalia peered down at the wound, *that must have been what had stung earlier.* "It looks worse than it feels, save the bandages for the others."

Mama Rose waved her hand, "We have plenty of those dear, and I think that you know by now that your Prince is a stubborn one when it comes to the people he cares for."

Erin made an agreeing noise in the back of his throat, "She's right, Jewel."

"Alright, but only if you promise that there are enough." She surveyed Mama Rose's features and deemed that the older woman was telling the truth.

Erin used the edge of his own shirt to wipe away the trail of blood before wrapping the cut securely.

"Come sit near the fire, you two. You'll be of no help to anyone if you get sick." Mama Rose patted Idalia's arm and walked towards the fireplace where the other twenty-three individuals huddled near the hearth.

Erin slipped his fingers through her own, stroking her hand with his thumb absentmindedly. The warmth that Idalia felt wash over her had nothing to do with the nearness of the inviting flames. They took a seat on the floor with a well-worn wooden bench to lean against and Idalia released a sigh of relief. "We did it." She said.

Idalia felt tension dissolve in his shoulder that she sidled up against, "We aren't out of the woods yet, but tonight went well." It sounded as if Erin was assuring himself along with her. Idalia shifted and laid her head on his shoulder, and Erin draped his arm across her side. "I couldn't do this without you." He whispered.

"Which part?" If Idalia knew him at all, then his words had a double meaning.

"All of it, life itself." She wished that he was aware of the skip in her heartbeat when he uttered those words.

It felt as if he could look directly into her heart with those warm brown eyes. Idalia wanted him to read every one of the thoughts that filtered through her mind at that moment, "I don't want to do life without you either."

Erin tucked a damp curl behind her ear and his fingertips lingered on her cheek. "Then it's a promise."

Idalia had always wanted to find her family. Some days, that desire was so strong that it overwhelmed her. Here, tonight, she realized that she'd found it in him. Erin had seen the best in her, when everyone else never could seem to see past the surface. The Prince had taught her that it was okay to wear her heart on her sleeve. She knew he would protect it. Not only that, but he had also enraptured it so fully that Idalia knew it could never belong to anyone else. So, she traced the line of his jaw with the back of her knuckles and replied, "You are everything that my heart has been missing."

Erin rested the side of his head against her own, and they stayed like that as Idalia let herself be lulled to sleep by the sound of the crackling fire and the mirth of those who thought they would never laugh again.

Chapter Thirty-Five
The Power He Holds

Erin awoke at dawn to the scuffle of Mama Rose coaxing the embers in the fireplace to curl back to life. He looked down to see Idalia peacefully sleeping with her head tucked against his chest. She must have shifted in her sleep.

The sight made his heart glow with warmth and flutter simultaneously. Mama Rose caught his eye with a knowing smile as she looked between the pair before she disappeared into the kitchen. It felt almost sacrilegious to wake up such an angel, but they had been there much longer than they should have.

"Rise and sparkle, Jewel." He chuckled as he brushed her hair from her eyes.

Idalia slit one eye open and then she slowly withdrew her arms from him. This left Erin feeling colder than he thought he would have been, especially with the fire so close by. "Oh no, I didn't mean to sleep for so long." She groaned as she rubbed the sleep from her eyes.

"It's a good thing that we did, we're going to need it." Erin stood to his feet and extended his hand to Idalia. They donned their cloaks once more now that the material was dried from the fireplace and nodded a goodbye to Mama Rose before they departed.

It had stormed for the majority of the night, and the signs were evident. Piles of debris were scattered all along the alley, and the remaining wind swirled dead leaves at their ankles. The rainwater puddles that they trudged through did nothing to soften the caked-on mud that had accumulated on their boots. The sky was still overcast, but at least now Idalia could see where she was going. However, this meant that others could also see them.

Erin tucked her behind him when they neared the gap in the Gate. The inside was silent, and Idalia thanked the Author that they had managed to arrive before the next rotation of guards. "Come on." Erin whispered and slipped through the curves of iron before pulling Idalia through. They had shed their cloaks in a bush and straightened their appearances so that if a guard were to see them, he would merely think that the Prince was out for a morning stroll with a lady friend. Now that it was just them, they had the assurance of a twisted form of safety.

"See?" Idalia swatted at the wind. "This is why we will have to plant flowering trees. Petals are much nicer to be assaulted with than brambles." Erin chuckled and helped to pluck the thorned plants from her sleeves.

"Except roses." She continued. "Roses I can handle." A playful grin lit up her features.

"Darling, I will string roses upside down so that the petals will fall as you walk." He leaned in and placed a kiss on her cheek, which he felt bloom with warmth under his lips.

"A chandelier of roses, perhaps?" Idalia gave him one of those smiles that could have made him forget his own name. She made him desire to be something better entirely.

"You deserve the entire ceiling." Erin nuzzled her nose and to his absolute delight, that drew out the sweetest laugh he had ever heard.

"I pity the gardener that would have to look after that many flowers." She shook her head as they stepped inside the palace.

"I was wondering where you went." A voice that made Idalia's skin crawl reached her ears and they both turned around.

"Is there a problem, Lester?" Erin subtly stepped in front of Idalia, to subconsciously protect her from his vile brother.

"I would like to speak with you privately, although perhaps I can spare a moment to escort the lady to her chambers?" Lester's gaze briefly roamed over Idalia, and she did not miss the spark of hunger that she saw residing in his dark eyes.

"I can escort myself." Idalia released Erin's hand and curtsied only to him, "Princes." She tacked on in lieu of goodbye before sparing Erin one last quick glance. Idalia heard their footsteps fade into the distance before she felt her arm tingle. There, etched on her skin in black cursive were three words. *I detest him.*

"Me too, Erin." She whispered to the air. "Me too."

Idalia did not escort herself back to the room, but rather slipped down into the prison to see how much headway she could make in convincing the remaining prisoners to leave with them. This was the first time she descended these stairs without Erin, but she no longer felt unsettled amongst the shadows that licked the walls. It seemed that every prisoner held their breath as she walked down their halls.

Perhaps they thought that whoever entered could be the one to make good on the promise of an impending end. Idalia knelt in front of Matthias's cell, but the man only stared straight ahead at the stacked stone.

"Matthias?" Idalia questioned. Perhaps he was so deep in thought that he didn't know she was there. "How are you?"

"Breathing." Was his mumbled reply.

Idalia's eyebrows furrowed in concern. The man before her felt like a husk of the one she'd come to know. "Has something happened?"

Matthias swallowed, but it appeared that the small motion put a strain on him. "I'm not myself lass, not anymore."

"If you're having a bad day, I promise it'll pass. It'll get-"

"Better?" Matthias interrupted with a grunted scoff but then his eyes met hers and he sighed. "If you're here to convince me to leave, I'm afraid you're wasting your time."

Idalia pulled her knees to her chest and interlocked her fingers around them. "Do you mind if I ask what changed?"

Matthias shifted, and the chains that bound his wrists scratched against the floor like the claws of an animal. "I can't say, for your sake." Matthias closed his eyes. "I'd like to be alone, lass."

Idalia nodded and rose to her full height. She would honor his wish to be alone, but something in her gut turned with unease. What could have happened? Perhaps Erin could talk to him and convince Matthias that a life outside of that cell would be much more rewarding than one within it. Several hours passed, and Idalia was able to successfully talk to five prisoners who changed their minds and decided to join the next group to escape. *"You can't force them;"* Erin had said once. *"Ultimately, they have the choice. We can only hope that they'll pick the right one."*

"Oy. You don't have permission to be down here." A guard that she did not recollect ever seeing before stalked over to where she stood. During her visit, the guards must have switched their rotation, and now three of them inhabited the hallway alongside her.

"Prince Erin gave me permission." Idalia raised her chin to hide the fact Erin had not told her that in so many words, but the guard didn't need to be aware of this matter.

The guard guffawed, "And why would he do that?"

"Are you questioning my judgement?" A rich voice laced with threat filled the stairway, and Idalia couldn't help but to fold her arms and give the guard a look that conveyed, *I told you so.*

"No. Of course not, my Prince." The guard swiveled on his heel and bowed low at the waist. "I was simply following protocol."

Erin surveyed the man, "Go bring me the rest of those in your rotation." He ordered and descended the last four steps.

"Right away, Your Highness." The guard dipped into a curt bow and snapped his fingers to get the attention of the other two men to follow him.

When they were gone Idalia whispered, "What are you doing?"

Erin released a controlled exhale, and the ghost of a smile that he gave to her was tight-lipped. "Trust me."

Shortly, seven men filtered into the prison and all bore the black and gray armor of a Gate guard. "We are all accounted for, Your Highness. How can we serve you?"

Erin swept Idalia's hand into his own and placed a kiss to her knuckles in an obvious statement. However, she did receive the unintended effect of a fluttering stomach at the gesture. Then he raised himself and turned to the guards.

"I give this woman the same amount of power that I hold. Whatever requests she makes, you are to honor. If the situation arises, you are to protect her. To betray her, is to betray my own crown. Kneel if you seal this vow." His caramel eyes darted to every single guard, as if watching to see if someone would show signs of refusal.

The sound of fists hitting metal rebounded through space as every guard knelt before their misunderstood Prince, and the girl who used to be their enemy.

Idalia could have sworn that Erin looked relieved.

Chapter Thirty-Six
To Mend a Heart

Erin and Idalia had done everything that they could to gather as many prisoners as possible into the group that would depart tonight. Unfortunately, half of them were still certain that to leave the prison was the equivalent of signing their own death warrant. They would be able to sneak ten souls out during this round, and Idalia could only pray that the rest would come to their senses because they were running out of time.

Unlike the first escape, Erin had to head up the second group to help shoulder the weight of a couple older prisoners who had unfortunately undergone Lester's torturous methods. That placed Idalia in the front. Perhaps fate decided to be kind to her because the full moon washed over the ground with its pale light, and she was certain that the winking stars were helping her to see as well.

As they started to silently venture out into the night, a rattling noise to her left nearly caused her heart to leap into her throat. They were about to be too exposed to whoever was making that racket if they continued around the corner. Idalia turned around and made several gestures to send her group stepping backwards.

There was that noise again.

No guard's footsteps would ever be that noisy. Or perhaps it only felt noisy to her ears because her thundering heartbeat was amplifying every sound. Idalia squinted, and she could barely make out the moonlit outline of a person on the other side of the Gate who was apparently trying to break in.

Idalia turned and whispered to the prisoner behind her to tell everyone not to step forward past the corner. The prisoner took light steps as she wove through the crowd to disperse the message. With that, Idalia took a risk.

As she got closer, Idalia realized that her guess had been correct, and she had to keep herself from audibly groaning. "What the Fates are you doing?"

Trevor whipped his head around to face her. "Oh Idalia, I've been so worried."

Idalia reached through the swirl in the iron and clamped her hand over his mouth. "Not so loud!" She said in a sharp whisper, and only after Trevor nodded did she pull her hand away.

"I came to get you. I know they kidnapped you and brought you back." Trevor spoke in a hushed tone, and she could almost hear him click his tongue as if to say, *You poor thing*.

They didn't have time for this. "Coming back was my choice."

Trevor balked, "You can't be serious."

Idalia wanted to throttle him, and if they were in a different situation, she just might have. "You should go." *Please, for the love of the Author, go.*

"Idalia-" Trevor clutched her hands through the Gate. "Come with me. We can leave this whole mess behind."

Idalia wrenched her hands away from his grasp, "And what about the war?"

"We'll run away. It's not our problem anymore." Trevor urged.

"That seems to be your favorite thing to do. You run away *every* single time something goes wrong." Idalia grit out. "It became my problem, a long time ago."

Trevor dragged a hand over his face, clearly frustrated with how this exchange was going. "Tell me this isn't because of that *Prince*." He all but spat out the word.

"This is because I've finally figured out where I am supposed to be, and it sure as the Gate is not with you." Idalia took a step backward.

"What is keeping you here? He is a monster and a wretched man." Trevor continued, as if he could win her over to his side by continuing to whisper-argue.

"He saved me when you wouldn't, and I'm better because of him."

She heard Trevor suck in a breath, and then there was silence for a moment before he leant into the curves of metal, "When you change your mind, come find me."

"That won't be necessary, Trevor. Now leave." Idalia pressed her palm to his chest and pushed him back. She heard him sigh as he shook his head and then the crunch of his boots on the dead grass slowly faded from her range of hearing. Idalia waited for a few more moments to ensure that he was truly gone before hurrying back to the group on silent feet.

"Are you alright?" Erin's moon-bathed features were pulled into a look of concern as he supported an elderly prisoner who already looked tired.

"Yes, it was just Trevor." She whispered. Idalia could have sworn that Erin frowned for a split second before the expression faded. "Let's go." She waved her hand to catch the attention of those in her group and they began their flight. Being in that dungeon for so long seemed to make each prisoner hold their breath with each step they took. The captives who had more years under their belts appeared especially wary of making noise even after the Gate began to recede from their lines of sight. While Idalia hated that their behavior stemmed from an innate sense of fear, it was a blessing, she supposed. It allowed for both groups to find their way to refuge.

After everyone had poured into the house, Erin tucked her to his side for a quick hug before he was pulled away to attend to another matter. Idalia made sure that the more senior ex-captives were comfortable before she looked over and found Erin laughing with a familiar little eight-year-old girl, balanced carefully on his hip.

"Angel-boy told you he'd be back, didn't he?" Idalia let out a light-hearted laugh, and the girl responded with a grin of mischievous excitement as she wrapped her thin arms around Erin's neck. He played along and pretended that the child was choking him. "Please, have mercy."

"Never." The girl cackled and Idalia couldn't help but smile at the sight. She was about to comment when a pair of voices made her ears perk up.

"Well, how many orphanages are there now?"

Mama Rose sighed, "Most of them closed down a while ago but Vincent, I highly doubt your daughter is still in one of them."

The man that Mama Rose was trying to console rubbed his hand over his scruffy jaw. Idalia recognized him as the one who had cried over the prospect of being able to go home to a daughter.

"She must think that we hated her." His shoulders that may have been broad once, now sagged in defeat. Something about the heartbreak in his voice made Idalia intercept.

"I'm sorry, Vincent, was it? I couldn't help but overhear, maybe I can help?"

Vincent nodded vigorously with a newfound sense of ambition. Idalia could only pray that she might be able to do something to keep his hope from dashing like glass to a stone. "Twenty years ago-" He swallowed, "We barely had anything for our little girl to eat. I had to do things I am not proud of to feed her, and I was punished for it." The most haunted expression that Idalia had ever seen crossed Vincent's eyes. "I don't know where she is, or if she even still lives in Thulta." The last part of his sentence came out quieter. As if he was just now considering the fact that his daughter may not be nearby at all.

Idalia drew in a breath, "I lost my parents around that time too. Maybe..." She thought for a moment. "Maybe we were sent to the same orphanage?"

Vincent dragged a hand through his hair, "Her name was Ruby. Is-" He closed his eyes. "*Is* Ruby." The way he repeated the statement made Idalia wonder if he simply wouldn't bring himself to consider the possibility that his daughter might be gone.

She couldn't recall anyone by that name from Miss Sarah's. Maybe she shouldn't have tried to block out that part of her life so fervently. "What did she look like?"

Erin had joined the small circle at some point in this conversation. Perhaps he could tell that Idalia was internally upset about being unable to help someone in a situation that felt so close to home and gravitated towards her.

"She had brown, curly hair and the sweetest brown eyes and more freckles than-" Vincent's voice broke, as if the memories were strangling him from the inside out.

"Take your time, sir." Idalia said gently. She couldn't help but wonder if this man's daughter knew how much she was clearly missed. How many nights had Idalia laid awake pondering if her parents had ever felt the same?

The next person to reply was not Vincent, but rather Erin murmuring something close to her ear. "Can I steal you away for a second?"

She nodded, "Excuse us, we'll be right back." Idalia bowed out of the conversation and let Erin pull her into the kitchen where a wall separated them from the crowd. "Do you think..." He started, and Idalia wrapped her arms around herself. "I don't know. Brown hair and eyes aren't exactly rare."

"I disagree, but I digress." He waved a hand. "Think about it, Love. He said that it's been exactly twenty years."

Idalia's gaze settled into his. "This is crazy." Her fingers hooked into the band that hung from her neck. "Erin, if we're wrong, it'll break that man's heart even more." She wasn't about to admit to herself that she was beginning to feel wishful at the prospect.

"And if we're right?" Erin's hand caressed the side of her arm. The sweet touch made Idalia feel steady even as the thoughts that barreled through her mind threatened to sweep her away with them.

"I'm not going to ask you to change me back. You've put enough of a strain on yourself as is." Her hand wrapped around his wrist.

"Darling, that's the least of what I would do for you."

Idalia leant forward and planted her forehead onto his chest. "When this is all over, you're taking a long nap."

The chuckle he gave reverberated through his chest like gentle thunder. "Come on, I'm about as impatient to see the real you again as he is." With that, Idalia felt the magic recede back into his palm. "You're definitely rare." A tender smile graced his lips.

"I'm already nervous. You're not helping, *Prince*."

Amusement and something else that Idalia didn't quite catch glimmered in his caramel eyes. "Stay here, I'll go get him."

Idalia took a shaky breath when Erin slipped away and dragged her fingers through her hair before quickly smoothing away the wrinkles of travel from her skirt. *Oh Author, could it be possible? After all these years?*

"Charlotte?" Vincent's eyes widened as he blinked back tears. "You-" He took a hesitant step forward. "You look just like her."

Idalia searched his eyes. Hazel, she realized. His nose turned down at the end like hers did. She tried to coax a word out of her aching throat. "Hi."

Vincent swallowed. "It can't be..." He studied her features and extended his arm in Idalia's direction. "Can I?"

Idalia nodded and closed the bridge between them as her father held her in his arms for the first time in twenty years. It was a hesitant embrace at first, as if they were still separated by layers of apologies and missed moments. Then, Idalia felt something stir in the corners of her memory. The way that her father cradled her form called to her heart like a beacon. Idalia had tucked that feeling away in the recesses of her mind without ever realizing it, and it wasn't long before his shoulder was dampened with her tears.

"I am so sorry, Ruby." He whispered, placing his hand on the back of her hair. "We never meant to leave you."

In his arms, Idalia was a child again. It felt as if that piece of her heart that had shattered was slowly fusing itself back together.

"I would have come for you if I had known." She clenched her eyes shut and her father loosed a shuddering breath before he pulled back from her.

"I want to hear everything. I want to know everything about you." Vincent squeezed her hands.

A laugh intermingled with a cry of happiness left her lips. "Let's sit down, I've waited so long to talk to you."

The pair found a small corner of the house that wasn't as alive with chatter. They didn't have much time and it would be difficult to fit a lifetime of stories into an hour, but Idalia was willing to try. Thirty minutes went by faster than she would have liked.

"Do you have a job, a family?" Her father leaned forward and rested his elbows on his knees. It looked as if he was not willing to let one more minute pass them by.

"I used to be a Sentry, but I regret that now." Idalia made a face that made Vincent chuckle. "And I'm not married, yet." Her eyes accidentally flicked to where Erin played with two children across the house. Her father followed her line of sight. "I'm sure I've long since lost the privilege to give you advice but if he's the one for you, then I support it." He smiled and the gesture felt so very familiar.

Most likely because it was reminiscent of the smile that she used to look upon in the mirror.

Idalia drew her knees to her chest. "I'd love to start again, Papa." Idalia tried out the word on her tongue, and Vincent's eyes turned glassy for a moment. "What happened doesn't change the fact that you're my father."

"You're as sweet as your mother." He reached out to take her hand and the question that had been burning on Idalia's tongue sprang forward.

"What happened to her, to mama?"

The feeling in the air rolled over into something heavy and heartbreaking. Like the moment before a soul gets crushed underneath the weight of their actions.

"We were both captured." He began, "The old Gate King put his prisoners through unimaginable mental torture. His son seems to prefer the physical type." Vincent shuddered. "Because I was the criminal, he took her from me and-" He had to wrench his gaze away and turn his head. "I never saw her again. It's been fifteen years."

Idalia had tried to make peace with the fact that she might not be reunited with her family. However, there was always a part of her that refused to let go of that kernel of hope within her grasp. Now that her father was back, it felt like reopening an old wound where she was forced to lose her mother again.

"Oh Papa," She breathed. "I'm so sorry that you had to go through all of that." Idalia glanced down at their joined hands.

"Ruby, I'm the one who should be apologizing. All we wanted was for you to have a better life and-"

"No." Idalia interrupted. "You gave *everything* for me. You both did."

"You turned out so wonderfully." Vincent said just above a whisper. "I'm so proud of you, sweetheart." Her father brushed away a stray tear that had trailed down the curve of her cheek.

Idalia held his hand close, willing herself to memorize everything about her father. From his voice to his eyes, to his words. Her gaze was drawn to Erin as he stood by the door, gathering their cloaks and folding hers over his arm. Idalia knew that Erin would give her as much time with her father as she wanted even though time itself was not in their favor.

"Stay here where you'll be safe for a while." Idalia stood to her feet and Vincent followed suit.

He wrapped her in his arms once more, "Promise me that you'll come back, one day."

"Of course, I will." She smiled.

"I love you, Ruby."

Idalia had waited so long to hear those words. Her father had sacrificed his all for her. "I love you too, Papa."

Vincent let go of her hands because this time, they knew that they hadn't lost each other. It is much easier to return to something found than something lost.

Erin saw her coming, and held the door open after handing Idalia her cloak. When they were outside, he smiled. "So?" An encouraging note in his voice begged her to share her thoughts.

Idalia did something better. She practically jumped into his arms out of sheer happiness.

"Oh!" He chuckled and spun her around with the momentum that she'd created. "I like this reaction."

"It *was* him, Erin. My father." She said breathlessly. "I still can't believe it."

"That's wonderful, Jewel." Erin set her back down on her feet but kept her close.

"I should have introduced you, why didn't you come over?" She tilted her head.

Erin chuckled, "You deserved to have that time alone with him, but don't worry, I want to meet him soon."

Idalia's hands slid down to rest on his chest, and she tilted her head back to look at the night sky. The breeze caressed her cheek and she was certain that tonight, every glowing star sparkled extra radiantly.

Chapter Thirty-Seven
A Wish To Last

"You know what I want to do?" Idalia set her hands on her hips once they'd re-entered the palace.

"What?" Erin gave her a curious smile.

"Let's go to Sylvie's Oasis. I want to end the night somewhere pretty."

Erin offered her his jacketed arm, "Then allow me to escort you somewhere pretty."

Idalia curtsied and slipped her hand over the crook of his elbow. It wasn't long before they found themselves at the entrance to the oasis and if Idalia strained her ears, she could hear the waterfall within.

"Ah, hold on, it's tradition." He dropped to a knee and Idalia let him slip off her boots so that she could feel every blade of grass underneath.

"We made a tradition?" Idalia remarked with a dash of playfulness as he set her shoes aside.

"Why of course, Jewel." Erin stood to his feet and took her hand, only to twirl her around. "The first of many, I hope."

Idalia flashed a bright grin and spun back into his chest where he promptly caught her by the waist and dipped her.

"See, this is the kind of impromptu ball I can get behind." Idalia laughed as they danced in time to the rush of the water.

"It's much more fun, isn't it." Erin winked as their dance called for them to pull apart for a moment only to collide back together. They were iron and fire, stars and night. The perfect complement in a world of missing pieces.

Erin and Idalia settled into a comfortable rhythm, gently swaying together amongst the fragrant flowers that hung down from the trees.

"Can I ask you something?" He questioned softly.

"Of course." Idalia smiled.

"I know you despise when people make assumptions about you, so do you mind if I love you?"

Idalia heard everything and nothing at the same time.

"What?" She squeaked.

"Do you mind if I love you? I do hope you don't, because I'm hopelessly too far gone." He murmured, brushing her cheek with the pad of his thumb as their dance came to a close.

"Please do." She whispered, "Because-" Idalia cradled the side of his face in her palm. "I love you too."

Erin rested his forehead against her own, and even the great waterfall couldn't drown out the sound of their adoring heartbeats.

"Aren't you glad you didn't end me with that bottle?" His voice took on a distinctly teasing note, all whilst remaining so warm, so open.

Idalia clicked her tongue as if she was considering it before she sighed in contentment. "Best decision of my life."

For a breath, the world had come to a standstill to allow them this moment. To offer them this ounce of time where they had only each other to consider.

Idalia wasn't sure how long such delicate perfection could last but she would have given anything to hold on for just one more heartbeat.

The Murmur

I knew that every second that went by was precious. That time spent together could have been the difference between what happened and what could have been, but she was much more precious.

I wouldn't have traded that night for all the second chances in the world.

Chapter Thirty-Eight
The Beginning of the End

Matthias had disappeared. Erin and Idalia stood in front of his newly uninhabited cell before their gazes met in silence. There was not enough scattered straw to dust the stone floor in a way that made it evident that a struggle occurred. It was as if Matthias had allowed himself to be led away without a fight, and that made the least sense of all.

"I don't get it." Erin's eyebrows drew together as he stepped into the cell. "He was here last night."

"Something was off last time I talked with him. I meant to tell you and then everything happened-" She sighed and pinched the bridge of her nose.

"You." Erin said abruptly, and Idalia's gaze snapped to his face only to find that his attention had been captured by two guards that descended the stairwell.

"Yes, my Prince?" Both men bowed to Erin, and then surprisingly, turned and did the same for Idalia. She could recall their faces from the small array of seven guards who had sworn fealty to them.

"The prisoner in this cell, where did you take him?"

Both guards exchanged puzzled glances. "We didn't, Your Highness." One man peered into the empty room and shrugged. "As far as I know, no one in our rotation moved him."

A muscle ticked in Erin's jaw. "Be sure to ask around, and report to me your findings."

"Of course, Prince." The two guards said in unison, and Erin stepped forward into the flickering lantern light, dismissing them with the tilt of his chin. As the guards strode down the opposing hallway, he turned to Idalia.

"Walk with me?"

Erin led Idalia to the overly large library that Lester had tricked her into visiting with him. The thought would have incited shivers to roll over her spine if it hadn't been for the more pressing questions on Idalia's mind. What happened to Matthias, and why had she not tried harder to help him when she could?

"What are we looking for, Love?" Idalia had to increase the speed of her steps merely to keep up with Erin's long strides. He was clearly on a mission, but the object of which was lost on her.

"This." He murmured as his fingers found purchase along the grooves of a heavy book laden with pages. Erin dropped it unceremoniously on a small table in the corner.

"And what exactly is this behemoth?"

Erin flipped through rows upon rows of writing. "If the guards didn't take him, then the only other explanation is that Lester had him tortured." A grim note had entered his voice, and when Idalia looked over his shoulder she realized that the many rows of text were not just words. They were names.

"He keeps a list of all who've been tortured?" Idalia asked, aghast.

Erin grimaced as his fingers slid over a column. "Only if they've met an end through his methods. It helps him keep track."

How awful, Idalia thought. *For a person's life to be reduced to a mere signature on paper whose only significance is to quench a ruler's insatiable thirst for bloodshed.*

"What if he isn't in there?" Idalia questioned, and Erin's eyes found hers for a brief second. "Then he's still alive."

Idalia could only hope that there was another explanation to all of this. However, if Matthias was still alive now, couldn't there be a chance that Lester was just in the process of torturing him?

"The names end here." Erin tapped the book with his index finger. "He hasn't been recorded."

"What do we do?"

Erin toyed with one of his rings, "Pray." He replied, as he slid the book back onto the portion of the shelf that was completely free from fine particles. That record was used so often, that dust was left little time to accumulate.

"We could have only helped him if he'd listened sooner. I can't demand answers or-" Erin swallowed, and she knew what he was refraining from uttering.

Idalia knew that it pained him to be unable to help a man that he considered a friend, but the pain would be unbearable if those hiding in Thulta were discovered.

They couldn't take those risks, no matter how badly they wished to.

"I'm glad I got to meet him." Idalia offered quietly as Erin tucked her to his side.

"I wish we could have done more." Erin sighed.

"You were a friend to him, Erin. If those were his last days, you made them worthwhile."

Erin's steps paused and he slid his gaze over to her.

"He was just too stubborn-" He shook his head. "We can only hope that we're assuming the worst."

Idalia nodded quietly in answer. She had always believed that it was incredibly easy to assume the worst in a place like this. However, the most beautiful diamonds form in the darkest spaces. One only needs to know where to look.

Chapter Thirty-Nine
A Moment of Glass

Erin left on an errand that night. While he was away, Idalia worked with the remaining ten prisoners. It wouldn't be long until the last wave of captives chose to forever leave this place.

As the hours ticked by, Idalia found herself becoming uncomfortably enveloped by her thoughts. She hated that her mind automatically conjured the worst possible scenarios that could contribute to why Erin was so late in returning.

Her fears were appeased when she stepped out of the prison and nearly collided with the caramel-eyed Prince.

"Well, hi there." Erin chuckled as he took her hand and intertwined their fingers.

"Where did you go? I was worried." Idalia cocked her head as she scanned his features. Erin peered over her shoulder to the looming pit in the floor and angled his head as a silent message to put some distance between them and any listening ears.

Idalia fell into step beside him and when he didn't answer her question, she nudged his side with her hip.

"I had a matter to discuss with Mr. Jameson." Erin gave her one of those smiles that made her knees wish to give out from underneath her.

"Mr. Jameson?" Idalia questioned. *That name was not ringing a bell.*

"Your father." Erin offered as he pushed open one of the double doors that led to the throne room.

Idalia made a small noise in the back of her throat in response. "Ruby Jameson... It feels so strange to say it." A hesitant smile turned into a soft laugh, because now she knew that she wasn't merely kidding herself by imagining about her family. She still had one. "I could have gone with you if you would have said something."

Erin's eyes glittered and he raised their interconnected hands to spin her around on the polished floor. "I told you I wanted to meet him. Besides, it was something I needed to do by myself, Jewel."

Idalia watched him with intrigue as she stopped herself from spinning by pressing a hand to a nearby column. "Alright, mister mysterious."

She looked around the room. It had a dark, lavish beauty to it that had always been both diluted and overpowered by Lester. Now when it was just her and Erin, Idalia thought that the space was quite lovely in its opulent demeanor. Pillars of black marble intertwined with veins of gold lined both sides of the room. The glass observatory-like domed ceiling gave them a perfect view of the night sky. From here, the stars looked like diamonds hung from glittering strings amidst a blanket of black velvet.

"Why do you call me Jewel?" She asked.

He took her hand in his own and led her up the darkened marble stairs before he spoke, "Don't you know that Jewels get set in crowns?"

With that, he had Idalia standing right in front of the throne, and she perched on the edge of it at the tilt of his chin. Erin dropped to a knee before her and bowed his head. "That is, if you want a crown."

She leant forward and swept a gentle hand underneath his chin, raising his head. "Only if you want a princess."

The brightest grin lit up his devastatingly handsome face, and he kissed her. The type of kiss that could only be shared by soulmates who despite everything, found each other. *Perhaps their story could be written down, and shared for years to come*, Idalia thought. She wanted proof that this moment was truly existing. That it was not just a favorite dream that she willed herself to cling onto with every one of her quickening heartbeats.

She felt its genuineness, in every softly murmured word he mumbled against her lips. Before she allowed herself to be enveloped in his embrace, she made out four unmistakable words...

My love. My queen.

Chapter Forty
The Glass We Shatter

"Is that why you went to my father? To ask for my hand?" Idalia's heart overflowed with warmth and affection for the man who held her hand as they ventured back through the palace.

"Aw, I guess I'm not mister mysterious anymore." He flashed her a smile and angled his head down to nuzzle her nose.

"No, but you are my fiancé." Idalia's voice took on a melodic tone.

"I do believe that's the best thing you can call me. Well, besides 'husband' eventually."

There had been several moments over the last several months that Idalia felt true, unhindered happiness flow through her. Tonight was her favorite moment, and any uncertainty about the future was pushed aside as her mind filled with daydreams and hopes. *About their future.*

At that moment, two guards stormed down the hallway towards them, wrenching Idalia from her fantasy. These must have been Lester's guards, from the way that daggers practically formed from their glares to be launched in Erin and Idalia's direction. Erin's hand tightened around hers.

"What is the meaning of this?" He slipped back into his Princely mask so fluidly, that if Idalia didn't know him, she would have gotten whiplash.

One guard halted to a standstill. Instead of replying, the foul creature spat on Erin's boots.

"What do you think you're doing?" Idalia clenched her jaw and forcefully shoved her hand into the guard's chest. The other man flexed and unflexed his hand, as if debating if he could get away with striking her with Erin so close by. The second guard sized both Erin and Idalia up, and unease began to churn in her gut.

"I thought I asked you a question." Erin stared him down.

Both guards exchanged a glance before they walked past, purposely shoving Erin's shoulder to the side. The one who had spat on him looked over his shoulder and said one word that made Idalia's world crack in half.

"Traitor."

She was certain that Erin had stopped breathing, and her own mouth had gone dry. He stayed rooted in the same position long after the guard's footsteps had faded into the shadows.

Then he readjusted his grip on her hand and pulled her behind him, before sweeping them both into a nearby room. Idalia wrapped her arms around herself as Erin pushed the door closed. His hand was shaking on the mahogany surface.

"Erin what do we-"

"You need to leave." He whispered, as if terrified of admitting his fear into the open air.

Everything crashed around Idalia like an overwhelmingly crushing wave. "What?" *He wasn't thinking clearly, surely...*

Erin turned to look at her, and the pain in his eyes alone was like a knife to her soul. He swallowed, "I would offer you the world if I could, but not this one-" His voice cracked, "What I can offer, is a better chance for your survival."

"What good is survival if you're apart from what makes you *want* to live?"

"And I can't live with myself if you die, when I could have prevented it!" His eyes turned wild, burning with the intensity of a roaring flame, but that flame was quickly extinguished as his shoulders sagged. "Please...I love you too much to have you with me."

He took a breath, shaky as it was and continued, "Go, cross this wretched gate, and marry him so that he can plead for you. Please." His strong hands gripped her shoulders, and she felt them tremble against her skin.

"We were so close." Idalia whimpered.

That seemed to make Erin's resolve falter, if only for a second. He pulled her into his arms for one last embrace.

"I'm sorry. I love you," He brushed the tears from her cheeks but a new one seemed to fall immediately in its place. "You have to leave, Darling." He whispered.

"Erin-" Idalia shook her head as she clamped a hand over her mouth to stifle the sobs. "I read the laws. If we do this I'll be banished. We won't-"

"I know." He looked between her eyes as tears slipped over his black lashes. "But you're so strong, You'll be okay. I-" He clutched the shirt material at his chest. "You'll be okay."

"There has to be another way, please." Idalia tried to wrap her arms around him, but he didn't let her. They both knew that if they gave in, they would never let go. Erin took a sharp, shaking inhale. It was the only thing keeping him from falling apart as he pressed down on the door handle and pushed it open.

"I will always love you." Idalia whispered as she stepped over the threshold. The small action severed something they knew they would never get back. Erin let his hand slip from her arm, and the missing touch opened a chasm underneath Idalia's feet that she was certain would swallow her whole and never release her.

Erin's glistening eyes reflected every bit of moonlight seeping in from the window. "Run, Idalia."

Oh, how badly she wanted to sink to the ground right then and there and beg fate to reconsider but somewhere, somehow, she found the strength to keep running. *How did everything go from being so perfect, to so wrong?* The only thing that could remotely ground her was the thumping sensation of his chained ring against her collarbone, as every step led her farther and farther from the one who had made her heart whole.

Now, it was utterly shattered.

The Murmur

*W*hen you love someone, you can't always keep them close. Watching her leave my arms felt the same as if my heart had been ripped out and skewered on a Gate spike, draining me of my life and resolve.

I miss her. My Jewel.

Chapter Forty-One
All She Never Considered

The only way for Idalia to refrain from collapsing into a heap of wracking sobs was to keep running. She would run until she reached Thulta, or until her legs buckled with the lead-heavy weight of her heartbreak. The seasons had begun to change over the past several months and now a whipping chill snapped over her exposed skin as her feet found purchase amongst the gravel and dirt. *This was it? This couldn't be it.*

Idalia had to stop. The Gate was far behind her and the idea of merely sagging up against one of the concrete buildings was much too appealing to ignore. Erin had thought her strong, but she didn't feel that way at all. *How could it all have been for nothing?* Idalia's shoulders shook as she crumpled against the façade of a shop. Crossing the Gate for the first time had been both the best and worst thing she could have ever done. The best, because she met

Erin. The worst, because now she could never be with him.

"Why?" Idalia craned her neck up to the sky. "What did we do to deserve this?" Idalia pounded her clenched fist against the rocky ground, causing the skin to split. "We were trying to fix everything." Her last words came out in a whisper as her tears slipped off her cheeks and watered the earth below.

Idalia finally had a taste of the life she had always hoped for, it was intoxicating and entirely too good to be true. It was all too cruel to be punished by way of impossible love.

Idalia's fingers latched onto the ringed necklace, completely ignoring the biting chill of the metal as it soaked up the cold around her. This was the only item she had from him, and it brought her enough courage to rise to her feet on unsteady legs. Erin had asked her for one thing, and she would go through with it. Idalia started to move in the wrong direction before realizing what she was doing. How long would it take before this tether towards Erin stopped tugging at her very core?

A shiver ran through her that could not be contributed to the wind as Idalia changed course and took one step, then two. It felt as if she was about to resign herself to a lifetime of watching events unfold around her while never being an active participant. It was a struggle to keep pace, but she willed her body forward.

Rows of shops and littered alleyways filled her periphery, blurry as it was. She walked down the familiar streets and up cobblestone hills graced with lampposts. It felt as if the world was breathing as slowly as she was. The fact that no one was here to share these streets with her only added to the growing pool of loneliness that Idalia waded through. But she continued. Towards the future she never wanted.

Towards Trevor.

Chapter Forty-Two
A Question for a Question

When Idalia rapped on the door of the Sentry compound, she felt the dull echo from her knuckles on wood reverberate into the growing cavern of her heart. Three knocks, and the door opened wide for her. Inviting her to a sort of imprisonment much worse than what she had believed she would encounter across the Gate. Idalia felt as if she was entering a cage of her own design as she locked eyes with Trevor. He took in her tear-stained cheeks and trembling shoulders with a pinched look of concern on his face.

"You're freezing, Idalia." Trevor took her hands and led her over to the crackling stove in the corner. The stove in question was a rickety old thing, but it did its job in providing enough warmth to flood the entryway. Idalia remembered a time when she first became a Sentry where stoking its embers had been a task they had given her in lieu of any real, meaningful work. She stretched out her fingers towards the heat, but it was as if the chill was emanating from deep within her gut and spreading outward to her limbs. It felt like fractals of frost on a window pane, how it spreads into every small crevice until one can no longer see out of the glass.

"What changed? I mean-" Trevor leaned against the wall, "Why did you come back?"

Idalia swallowed, "I had to." She withdrew her hands from the vicinity of the stove and buried them underneath the folds of her skirt. "I got into some trouble."

Trevor slumped down to the ground beside her, "Did he hurt you?"

Idalia's eyes flicked to Trevor's in an instant, and the fire in them could have rivaled the burning coals in the stove. "Of course not." She snapped.

Trevor's eyebrows raised, "I'm sorry, I just... You're not giving me a lot to go off of here."

Idalia sighed sharply. If this was going to work, she had to reign in her emotions. "I was involved in something that... went too far." Her gaze dropped to her feet. She had to be so very careful with her words with him. It was like stepping around shards of glass.

"What happened?" He lowered his voice even though the compound was nearly silent now that the rest of the Sentries were asleep.

Idalia took a moment to gather her thoughts before she slowly launched into a version of her story that had many omitted details. She told him a fictitious version of the events, beginning with someone that Idalia had met and befriended in the Gate and ending with them both being found out. "So, I had to escape." She lied.

Trevor stared into the flickering stove and pressed his interlocked hands to his lips. "Why didn't you tell me? I could have helped you get that person out."

Idalia wanted to roll her eyes, or shake him in frustration, but she did neither. "It was just such a whirlwind; besides you were busy with the war." Idalia had to tear her eyes from his face as she said the last part of her sentence.

"But you're safe now that you left?" Trevor searched her expression for confirmation.

Idalia shook her head but before she could get her next words out, a shudder ran through her. Each sentence spoken was one closer to the inevitable most dreaded use of her voice.

"Hold on, let me make you something warm before you go on." Trevor pushed himself to his feet and walked away. Idalia cupped the ringed necklace in her hands and looked at it. She had fallen for Erin, and he had caught her in every way one could be captured. Now, Idalia was doing a different type of falling entirely. The kind that came with those dreams where gravity seizes your body and pulls you down into a vast expanse of black nothingness. The difference was that people always wake up from those dreams with a start and a thundering heartbeat. How would she claw her way up if she made contact with the bottom of that abysmal canyon?

Something shattered from the kitchen that sounded vaguely like a glass cup. *Like a glass bottle.* The memory of their first meeting tortuously flashed in front of Idalia's eyes, causing them to water.

"I'm sorry, I didn't mean to startle you." Sympathy flooded Trevor's voice as he knelt down in front of her and handed over a wooden bowl filled with steaming soup.

Idalia stared at it, not even bothering to wipe away the fresh tears that rolled down previously laid tracks.

"The things you must have gone through there." Trevor whispered and shook his head, patiently waiting until she took the bowl from his hands.

"Did you mean what you said?" Idalia said just slightly louder than a whisper. "About leaving this all behind and running away?"

Trevor blinked at her, "Yes..." The hesitancy in his voice made Idalia wonder if he hadn't counted on her accepting the offer. But it had been there, and she had no choice but to agree to it.

"I'm not safe here." She responded to his earlier question, "I have to leave Thulta."

Trevor loosed a long exhale. "And you want me to come with you?"

Idalia set the bowl on the floor to her right. "Yes." *Lie, Lie, Lie.* Her own mind shunned her tongue. "But it's not just that."

"You can say whatever you need to. I let you down once, I'm not going to do that again." He slipped her hand into his larger one and the touch felt so foreign that Idalia had to refrain from yanking her wrist away. She took a deep breath and uttered four words that she knew she'd regret forever.

"Will you marry me?"

Chapter Forty-Three
One Wedding Bell

The only minister that they could find at that early hour was a portly fellow with a suffocatingly overbearing wife. Idalia wasn't sure how she would go through with this. She could barely get a word out for fear that her throat would close up with the crushing weight of her repressed cries. It still hadn't sunk in as reality when Trevor had nodded his reply a mere few hours before.

"Aw." The minister's wife tutted, "It's always such a beautiful sight when the bride gets all teary." The woman tugged a small veil over Idalia's hair and turned her to look at her reflection in the small golden mirror that hung on the wall of the minister's home. Her eyes were bloodshot, but her complexion should have been much splotchier from all her crying. *It should have been.* Erin's magic still had a hold on her body, and she would be reminded of him each time she saw herself in any reflective surface.

Perhaps it should have given her some sense of twisted assurance. As long as she still looked this way, that meant Erin was alive and well. Did that mean he could still feel her in some way? Idalia would have given anything to feel a prickling sensation along her forearm. To look down and see a cursive message inked along her skin. The message never appeared. He truly was letting her go.

Idalia didn't remember the walk between rooms in the minister's house. She didn't pay much attention as she walked through their foyer holding a single moonflower that the minister's wife had plucked from their flowerbed. Before she knew it, she and Trevor were face to face.

The only way that Idalia could manage was if she imagined that the calloused hands holding hers belonged to Erin. If she tried, Trevor's voice could deepen and soften and turn into Erin's melodic tone but no matter how hard she wished, when she opened her eyes, the man before her was not the one she loved.

"Do you, Trevor Carlisle, take this woman to be your lawfully wedded wife?"

Trevor dipped his chin to affirm, "I do."

The minister turned to her, "And do you, Idalia-" He paused, as if he now realized that he was unaware of her maiden name. Idalia took a breath; she *had* a last name now. It would be so easy to utter it, but what gave her pause was the fact that her father's name was her past. It was a past that she had longed for, yes, but she was no longer a woman of times gone by.

Even though this wasn't the future she wanted, Idalia would hold on to what might have been. What she desired more than anything.

"Amias." Idalia offered.

The rotund man gave a grunt of acknowledgement and shoved his spectacles further up the bridge of his nose. "Do you, Idalia Amias, take this man to be your lawfully wedded husband?"

Idalia swallowed the lump in her throat and willed herself to breathe. She was thinking of the caramel-eyed Prince of the Gate and him alone, as she said, "I do."

Chapter Forty-Four

A Different Time, a Different Place

The silver band on her ring finger weighed Idalia's hand down as she fastened a pack to the saddle of her new horse. It felt so at odds with the golden one that lay tucked underneath the neckline of her white shirt. Trevor had bargained with a stall owner amongst the early morning mist for the mare in exchange for several of his weapons. The mood of the day seemed to align with Idalia's. Dreary and bleak, with a hint of a storm in the air.

"This is it." Trevor secured the buckle of one of the saddlebag straps and looked at Idalia. "Do you want to…" He gestured to the saddle and Idalia shook her head. "I'd rather walk for a little bit."

Trevor gathered the horse's lead and they started towards the road that would lead them out of Thulta. Away from everything and *everyone* she loved.

"This is kind of wild, isn't it?" Trevor spoke up, clearly trying to distract her from her thoughts.

"What is?" Idalia pulled her hair back with a cord of twine.

"This." Trevor gestured to the horse and their small amount of belongings and the journey ahead of them. "I'm still coming to terms with the fact that we just got married." He gave a half chuckle and shook his head, causing his tawny hair to slip into his eyes.

Idalia made a non-committal noise in the back of her throat and let her eyes wander. The crunch of gravel underneath their boots and the clopping of horse hooves sounded vaguely like the drumming beat that sometimes accompanied an impending war. They crossed to the top of a hill where the dirt road evened out by the tracks of many travelers going to and fro. From this vantage point, Idalia could nearly see it all. Her eyes caught onto the streets she had patrolled and grown up running through, the many buildings that had blurred into the background as she went through her daily life. Idalia should have paid them more attention, she supposed. To remember more details about something was better than to not remember it at all.

Then there was the Gate in all its dangerous wrought iron wonder. The sunrise that crested over the hill set the metal on fire, glinting off of the curves in a mix of black, gold, and burning orange. Idalia had never noticed the beauty of it before. It was a deadly work of art that called to her conscience in a way that would be forever hard to ignore.

So maybe she could give it her attention one last time.

"Trevor." Idalia halted in her tracks, and he stopped along with their horse.

"Hmm?"

"I-" Idalia bounced on her heels. "I forgot something, I need to get it."

Trevor gave her a confused look, "Idalia I thought you said time was of the essence."

"It is." She assured him, "But I can't leave without it." Idalia turned and sped down the hill, "I'll be back." She called over her shoulder as her feet carried her towards the one place her heart so longed to be. Idalia tore through the branches and stepped over tumbled rocks until she found the opening in the Gate. *Welcome home.* It seemed to say as Idalia slipped through and nearly fell over her own boots when her eyes landed on his form. *Erin.*

He looked... Idalia pressed the back of her hand to her mouth. He looked so pitifully broken. She could see it in his stride, in his shoulders, and in the sullen expression on his features. Idalia felt heartbroken, Erin looked it. Then she saw him reach a hand up to his temple and it came away stained red.

Idalia held her breath and approached him from behind.

"I leave you alone for a day and you get into all kinds of trouble."

Erin whipped around with wide eyes and his lips parted in surprise. It was as if he didn't want to fool himself by believing that she was truly there. "Jewel." His voice was hoarse, and then she saw tears gather at his lash line. "Oh my-" He pulled Idalia into his arms for that hug that they didn't allow themselves when they should have. "You can't be here."

"I couldn't leave without seeing you one more time." She stepped back from their embrace to look at him. He had a wound that dripped crimson over his cheekbone and down the side of his face. "What happened?"

Erin glanced down at his hand that was still sporting the transfer of blood from a moment ago. "I got the last ten out. But two of them were good actors and they instigated a fight." Erin shrugged it off as if he barely felt the gash. Idalia reached her hand up to try and brush the strands of his hair away from it, but Erin drew in a sharp breath, and she halted. His eyes tracked to the glint of the silver wedding band on her finger, and he took a step back. Idalia brought that hand close to her chest. Erin gave her the saddest smile she'd ever seen.

"I should have held you for longer, now I don't have the right to."

"Erin-" Idalia murmured, "It's already killing me to leave you, please don't say you can't hold me."

"You're not mine, Love." With a gentle touch, Erin reached out and brushed the tears away from her lashes. "But I'll always be yours."

Idalia clutched his hand close to her, as if she could memorize the exact weight and feel of it to carry around with her for the rest of her life. Erin shuddered, and she didn't have to look up at him to know that his tears fell in sync with her own.

Whether it was fate, the stars, time, or the Author; something was allowing them these last heartbeats together. They would be two people forced to go in separate directions on paths that could never converge again. They had already broken so many rules, and all Idalia wanted was to break one more.

So she pressed her lips to his own. There were so many unspoken messages in that kiss. A goodbye, an "I love you," and an apology.

They shouldn't have closed their eyes.

Because when they opened them, they were surrounded by twelve guards with swords drawn who had crept up to them on silent feet.

"You are under arrest for treason against the Gate." One of them commanded through his helmet. "As ordered by his Highness, Prince Lester."

The Murmur

I was no stranger to nightmares. In fact, I was often plagued by them. But this was even more horrible because I had brought her into one of them and I had no way to get her out in time. I'll never forget the look she gave me at that moment. A complete and utter surrender of her trust.

Given to the man who loved her enough to destroy her life.

Chapter Forty-Five
Too Late to Run

S hackles snapped around Erin and Idalia's wrists. The cuffs themselves had serrated edges like teeth that dug into the skin with any slight movement. Any attempt to wrestle their hands free could result in permanent scarring. The guards roughly shoved them forward, and Idalia heard one of them chuckle when Erin stumbled after a particularly forceful push.

"Not so high and mighty anymore are you?" He sneered, and the doors to the grand throne room were cast open like the mouth of a fabled monster who waited to swallow them whole. Lester stood in front of the throne, a cruel smile contorting his mouth. He gestured for the guard that held Erin's chains to bring him closer, while Idalia was forced to stay in one place. Her heart thundered in echo with each one of Lester's calculatingly slow footsteps towards Erin and she tried to thrash out of her captor's hold. The man grunted and jerked the shackles around her wrists so that razor-sharp pain lashed up her arms and she let out a small cry of alarm. Erin's head snapped towards Idalia, "Don't touch her." His voice dropped into a venom-laced snarl.

"I don't think you're in a position to command them, dear brother." Lester watched Erin with a level gaze.

"Your quarrel is with me, not her. Let her go." Erin's tone was unwavering.

"Did you think you were smart?" Lester cocked his head.

Erin clenched his teeth. "What are you referring to?"

Lester chuckled and rubbed a thumb over his jaw. "I noticed that my dungeons were looking a little... light." He spoke thoughtfully, "At first, I thought you were carrying out your tasks. Like the good puppet that you are." Lester leant towards his brother. "But there were never any bodies." Lester motioned for Erin's shackles to be removed on his right hand and Idalia breathed an imperceptible sigh of relief until she noticed that the chains were replaced by Lester's own vice-like grip.

"So I got curious." Lester made eye contact with a fearsome guard in the corner and an unspoken message passed between them as the nasty-looking man approached and seized Erin's other arm behind his back. Erin gritted his teeth and tried to wrench his body away unsuccessfully.

"Did you know," Lester continued as he produced a gleaming Blackstone dagger from a sheath tucked close to his waist. "That you've been watched? The last two times that you went through with your pitiful smuggling attempts?" Lester pulled Erin's wrist forward and brought the dagger to his skin. "Not everyone was daft enough to follow you though." The vile Prince smiled. "In fact, I wouldn't have caught word of all your betrayal if it hadn't been for that one... Matthias? Was it?"

Idalia drew in a breath so sharp that it hurt her lungs. *No. Matthias would not have betrayed them...*

"Lester." Erin warned, and Idalia saw his entire posture stiffen to resemble one of the stone pillars that surrounded the room as Lester pressed the tip of the dagger into the top of Erin's wrist and he winced.

"You tried to siphon my power away, Erin. Now it's my turn." With that, Lester slashed through Erin's skin, tearing apart veins and nearly sending him to his knees from the agony. A scream flew from Idalia's mouth, but Lester paid her no mind.

The large guard reclasped those wretched bonds onto the wrist that dripped blood and the serrated teeth only dug further into his raw flesh. Then the process was repeated over again. "There. Matches your bleeding heart." Erin writhed against his captor with rapidly dwindling strength. He groaned as the blade severed through the very vein that magic had pulsed through just minutes before. His complexion was pallid, and the light that always shone outwards from his eyes was starting to blink out.

"Stop!" Idalia begged. "You're killing him!" She saw red, and slammed her heel down as it made contact with her detainer's foot, and he let out a cry when a very satisfying crunch reached her ears. The guard moved backwards, releasing her chains and she didn't waste one moment to rush to Erin's side. Idalia had nearly reached him when his body was thrown to the side against a marble pillar and the most strangled noise wrenched itself from his throat as his ribs took the brunt of the impact. Idalia's arms were once again pulled behind her by a guard she did not know. She kicked and screamed but it was to no avail. Lester watched the scene contently, as if their misery brought him entertainment. Idalia looked at Erin, and to the small pool of crimson that was beginning to collect where his hands had fallen. "I'm sorry." He whispered. Erin tried to push himself up, and when that did not work, he tried to cling onto the tether of his magic with anything he had left.

But he had nothing left.

Idalia gasped as what felt like ice water crashed over her body, chilling her from the inside out. The hair that fell over her shoulders as she thrashed was no longer black, it was brown. The skin that was tearing underneath her cuffs was not the subtle color of moonlight, but the tanned tone of a Thultan. Lester's eyebrows flicked up as recognition shifted his features into something horrific.

"*You.*"

Erin's moan of excruciating pain was not lost on her ears as he strained to reach her, but as he tried, a heavy boot was thrust into his back, and he crumpled yet again.

A hissing laugh trailed over Lester's lips, and he snapped his fingers before wrapping them around the stem of a goblet. Immediately, more guards filtered into the room, and Idalia's stomach tumbled as she recognized some of their faces.

"Kill her and make him watch." Lester ordered.

No, oh Author please don't make him watch.

"Please!" She cried, begging for any of the guards to remember the vow that they had sworn to them.

Not a single armored man stepped forward to both her hope and dismay.

"Are you enjoying the scenery?" Lester snapped.

Phineas cleared his throat and stood taller. "We took an oath, to protect to this woman."

Lester swirled the blood-red liquid in his goblet. "You swore an oath to my brother's plaything. You did no such thing for this miscreant."

The guards shifted glances between each other, and Idalia felt her hope plummet like the tears that freely splashed on the black marble floor.

"Do whatever you want with me." Idalia spat, "But let him live."

Lester leaned forward on his throne, "I did offer you a chance once, and I am not in the habit of handing out second chances."

"She's-" Erin whispered hoarsely, "Married." He clutched his screaming ribs. It looked like every breath he took sent him into a new type of hell.

Lester's eyebrows furrowed, "The plead? Oh, little brother, you're a sneaky one."

Idalia brought her bound hands to her mouth to stifle a sob. *He knew all along that this would happen.* The marital plead was Erin's only assurance that she could keep her life.

"Send for him." Lester said to someone in the far corner, but his gaze never left Idalia's.

"In the meantime, lock them both up. I heard of this delightful little compound in Thulta, Erin I do hope you don't mind if I pay them a visit."

Erin gritted his teeth and tried to lunge for Lester, but the fearsomely large guard grabbed his chains and yanked on them backwards with enough force to separate body from bone.

Idalia nearly vomited at hearing the crack that reverberated from his body before he slumped to the marble, unconscious.

Idalia was screaming, she didn't know when she started or how to stop. All she knew was that she had to get to Erin. She didn't see the guard behind her that advanced at the flick of Lester's wrist. She only felt the impact of the blunt object that he used to send her to the same fate as the man she loved.

The Murmur

S he didn't stir as she slept, despite every horrific thing that had just unfolded. I couldn't reach the place that she had gone. This distance, this gap between us seems to span across continents when we are only a couple feet apart.

If she slips away, she will take me with her.

Chapter Forty-Six

To Return the Favor

I dalia awoke to a high-pitched ringing in both of her ears. Her head felt cloudy with a sharp pain pressing on the barriers of her skull as if it desperately wanted to break loose of its confinement. As her vision slowly came back into focus, she took note of her surroundings; a dingy cell with a hay-scattered, slimy floor and the faint scent of mildew.

Erin.

Where was he? Idalia forced her limbs to obey and lift her from this miserable floor before her fingers latched around the jagged iron door. It bit into her palms, but the sensation was overpowered by the way her heart seized as her gaze fell upon the bloodied Prince. "Erin!" She cried and tried to stick her hand out of the cell.

Her plea snagged the attention of a guard who stood rigidly in front of Erin's cell. "He can't hear you, miss." The man spoke. She recognized him. He was the one that brought her to Erin that night when she fled the compound.

"Let me get to him." Idalia ordered, and when the guard did not move, her countenance faltered. "Please."

The man sighed and glanced over his shoulder to the unconscious Prince. "I was given orders to keep you both separated."

Idalia shook her head vehemently. "No, please. I'm not asking to be set free, just imprison me with him!" She pounded her hand into the cell door to keep the man's attention, and her blasted wedding ring banged against the metal with a sharpness that ricocheted through the space.

The guard rubbed his stubble covered jaw with a gloved hand, "I don't think-"

"You swore an oath to us. To me." Idalia tried to draw herself up taller. With every wasted second, Erin was edging closer to death's door.

The armored man hesitated, "I know, my lady but-"

"Allow me three requests." Idalia blurted. She should have asked for more, but if he agreed, she could make three work.

The guard dipped his chin. "To honor the oath that we swore, I will grant them."

Idalia exhaled in relief. "First, let me into his cell." She took a step back from the door as a sign that she wouldn't instigate a fight with the man. The guard grabbed a ring of black iron keys and inserted one of them into the lock before twisting it and ushering Idalia out. He repeated the same action with Erin's cell, and Idalia fell to her knees beside his slumped form.

They only had a few torches along the hallway that cast both light and shadows into their confined area. But, it was enough for Idalia to see how painfully pale Erin was turning. She cupped his face in her hands. His skin was clammy, and his clothes were stained with his own blood. She drew in a gasp as she saw how his arm hung unnaturally from its socket.

Idalia heard the guard hiss between his teeth as he truly took in Erin's state. "That needs to go back in."

"Can you help me reset his shoulder? I'll make sure to keep him still." She met the eyes of the guard.

"Is that your second request?" His hand rested on the hilt of his sword. *Author, she should have thought this through.*

"Yes." Idalia swallowed and moved to Erin's other side to give the guard room. She held the Prince's other hand

and was met with the sensation of the slickness of cooled blood that had dripped from his wrists into his palm. His typical scent of a crackling fire and spiced apple cider was now intertwined with the metallic tinge of spilled coins. The man sighed and set Erin's limp form fully flat on the ground before he carefully eased his arm away from his body at an angle before pulling at the limb in a way that slid the bone back into its rightful place with a heavy click.

Erin groaned. As soon as Idalia started to prop his head up, it lulled to the side in her hands. "You're going to be okay, sweetheart." She whispered and looked up at the guard. "Thank you. I'm ready for my last request."

The guard rose to his feet and brushed the straw from his pants. "What is it?"

"I need clean water and bandages." Idalia said hurriedly as she brushed Erin's bangs away from his forehead. Beads of sweat clung to his hairline and his eyes darted underneath his eyelids with a feverish pace. The guard made an acknowledging noise and stalked off to grant her request.

"You've fought for so long." Idalia murmured, "I need you to keep fighting for a little longer."

What felt like an eternity was merely ten minutes before the guard knelt beside her with three bowls and a bundle of cloth. "You'll need one to give him drink." He pushed one bowl that sloshed water over the sides of its rim towards her. Idalia nodded her thanks and the guard turned away from the couple to lock their cell-door. Idalia eased Erin's head into her lap and held the bowl to his lips. She would have given anything for him to look up at her and greedily wolf down this water, but it only trickled between his parted lips.

Idalia held his left arm with the tenderness of a mother holding her infant child and dipped a rag into the other bowl. He didn't even flinch as she worked to wipe the crimson away that seemed to stain everything. "I know you're tired, but please don't go to sleep forever." Her voice broke as she surveyed his serrated skin. The wounds had stopped gushing blood, but what if he'd already lost too much before she had been able to get to him?

The gashes needed to be stitched up, but she had nothing to use. For now, she could only pray that she could secure these bandages tightly enough to matter.

Idalia noticed something with his wrists. The slashed wounds were deep, but Lester had intentionally dragged the dagger a certain way. From where Idalia had been standing, it looked like the vile man had lacerated Erin's skin in a sole desire to make him hurt. Lester hadn't cut him with the intention to kill him, but to destroy his essence from the inside out. He wanted his brother to suffer in silence. The type of agony that no one else could understand and that he could never explain.

The magic that Erin used to carry had supported him as a sort of life-force for all these years. It was evident that his body didn't know how to compensate for the lack of what had always been a certainty. With both wrists cleaned and bandaged, Erin started to shiver. Idalia took his hand in her own and held it to her heart.

Then Erin's body went still.

"You aren't allowed to leave me." She choked. "I would have been your Queen, surely that has some power." A single tear dripped from her cheek and landed on his chest.

"You were... engaged to danger." He rasped. His voice sounded like sandpaper that had been trampled on, but his eyes were slowly opening to look at her. *Thank the Author.*

Idalia's shoulders shook as a relieved laugh mixed with a sob overcame her. "Are you okay?"

Erin closed his eyes again. "Something's broken," he brought his hand up to rest on his chest. "It doesn't feel... right."

Idalia placed her hand on top of his, and as gently as she could muster she spoke, "Your magic is gone, Love."

A heavy sigh slowly pulled itself from his lungs. Then he murmured, "I'm sorry."

Idalia's eyes softened, "Why on earth should you be sorry?" She dragged the back of her knuckles along the silhouette of his face.

"You came back for me." He swallowed, "I couldn't protect you."

Idalia lowered her face to rest her forehead on his own.

"But you did, Erin." She said softly, "You let me go to save me."

He reached up a bandaged hand to curl a lock of her hair around his finger as if he were trying to memorize each individual strand in the dark. "You can still get out of here if he comes for you."

Idalia shook her head silently, "I won't go with him."

Erin's muted caramel eyes fell into hers. "You have to. This isn't the life I want for you, Jewel."

Idalia sniffed and wiped the dampness from her cheeks before pushing her shoulders back with determination. "*You* are the life I want. No matter how long or short it may be." In that moment, sitting on the floor of a grimy cell in the pit of the Gate, and holding one of its Princes, Idalia looked every bit a Queen.

"Idalia…" He breathed her name like a prayer. A plea to keep her close, but close couldn't mean safe.

She pressed her finger to his lips. "Whatever happens, I want to share your fate."

Erin took a shaky breath, "I knew I'd fall in love with you from the beginning. I've never run towards anything faster."

The softness in his eyes offset the dried trickle of crimson at his brow. Despite his disheveled and pained appearance, Idalia thought he'd never looked more handsome. An angel with broken wings, but an angel, nonetheless.

"I love you." She whispered.

Idalia didn't know what fate awaited them, but she knew that there was no one else that she'd want to share these last moments with. That's all life was. A series of moments. There are some good, and some bad. If you're fortunate, you'll find someone to love you through it all.

Erin and Idalia savored this moment of calm before screaming echoed through the castle.

Chapter Forty-Seven
So It Begins

The war. The Sentries were attacking.

"Help me up." Erin gritted his teeth as Idalia pulled him to his feet. He swayed on his heels and Idalia reached for his waist to steady him before a hiss of pain escaped his lips.

"Sorry!" She winced.

"No-" His hand drifted to his ribs.

Idalia's gaze roamed over the area that his hand was currently pressed against. "Are they broken?"

"I think so-" Erin's words were abruptly cut off by a horrendously startling clatter that reached their ears from above the prison.

The guard that had helped Idalia drew his sword and started towards the staircase but then he stopped in his tracks and looked back at their cell. He sheathed his sword momentarily to snatch the key ring from the iron hook nailed to the wall and threw the keys into their cell.

"Your Highness." The man bowed at the waist and dashed to the stairs.

Idalia felt a surge of gratitude towards the guard as she grabbed the keys and shoved open the door that held them captive.

A cacophony of roared voices thundered overhead, and Erin grabbed her wrist. "We need a plan."

"We need to stop Lester from getting to the compound."

"And convince the Sentries to end this." Erin added as they headed for the exit.

"The Esterod soldiers won't listen to us, but Trevor may be able to convince them."

"Lester's guards will be distracted; I should be able to get him alone." A muscle ticked in Erin's jaw as they ascended each step. He was in no state to fight, but they didn't have a choice. When they surfaced into the open, she saw the bodies that were already scattered across the marble floor like poppies dotting an otherwise barren field.

Erin turned his head away, just long enough to steel his resolve before he knelt to the side of a fallen guard with a grunt of discomfort and snatched his weapons.

This was her fault.

No. Idalia fought her guilt. *The fight between good and evil is a battle that's been stirring for millennia. We are only the catalysts.*

Erin tossed her a sword as she tore the fabric of her skirt away so she could fight. The cream material now stained by the filth of the dungeon and the blood of the fallen, swished in tattered ends around her shins. "Go." Idalia allowed herself one last look into the eyes of her beloved before she tore down the corridor, all the while praying under her breath that he would be alive when she returned.

Chapter Forty-Eight
Time Is Finite

Clang! Idalia's sword countered with one of an Esterod soldier who had been two heartbeats away from driving his blade into the heart of a cowering servant.

"Stop it, girl." He growled, and exerted more effort into the force of his blade which nearly knocked her backwards, but Idalia remained upright.

"There is no need to kill her." She gritted her teeth and used his distraction to sweep the man's feet from underneath his body. His head cracked against the wall, and he slipped into a heap. The huddled servant muttered her fervent gratitude, but Idalia didn't have the luxury to respond or even reassure the woman.

She had to find her husband.

Idalia rounded the corner and was greeted with a hundred soldiers beginning to pour into the heart of the Gate. She stifled a gasp and ducked behind a pillar. Their nearing footsteps pounded in rhythm to her heart and acted as a countdown to the time they were desperately running out of. The soldiers were everywhere, and she looked exactly like a fugitive.

Idalia had to wrench her gaze away from the bloodied bodies as she sped through the halls. It was a massacre, and she couldn't stop long enough to decipher whether the dead belonged to the Gate or the Sentries.

A body was a body, and right now, it was a horrible free for all. Idalia's lungs burned along with her legs, but she would not give in to the demands of her limbs and the cramping of her muscles.

"You!" A man stormed towards her, flipping a dagger in the air and catching it with dangerous precision. A cruel smirk twisted his mouth, "It's a pity to end such a pretty thing, but I'd rather get paid." His knife sliced the air towards her, and Idalia lunged backwards. "I don't have time for this." She said flatly. The man was fast, but he was also cocky, and Idalia could use that overconfidence to her advantage. Idalia twisted her wrist in a way that forced her sword to act as a gleaming barrier between her collarbone and his dagger. The soldier raised his hand and landed a blow to the side of her head. Idalia saw stars and blurry dots spread across her field of vision, but she blinked them away as rapidly as they appeared. The soldier produced a low chuckle, and he pressed the tip of his blade to Idalia's throat. "You're a little more of a nuisance than I gave you credit for."

Idalia gulped. *Take me for granted*, she thought. *It's served me well so far.* She slipped on a mask of trepid fear and once he smiled, she drove her knee into his groin.

The soldier cursed at her and fell to his knees. His howls of pain followed Idalia down the next hallway. Idalia gulped down air to satiate her needy lungs as her legs carried her along the outskirts of this battle.

A left, a right, another left.

She had taken so many turns and yanked herself behind more pillars than she could count when more soldiers stomped by, oblivious to her presence.

Idalia's furious haste skidded to a halt when she realized that there was one door that was not supposed to be ajar.

The entrance to Sylvie's Oasis was open, and in its center, stood Trevor.

Chapter Forty-Nine
Our True Colors

"Trevor, what are you doing?" Idalia's tone bordered on apprehension, and Trevor shook his head.

"Was this what you forgot, Idalia?" His gaze slid over her reverted appearance.

Idalia let her sword rest against her leg as she took strides towards him. "Trevor we don't have time, this war has to end."

Trevor raised his eyebrow and rolled the sleeves of his shirt up. "Oh it will end, just not in the way you're hoping." His gaze softened. "Can't you see, Idalia? He's been lying to you. Do you hear that?" Trevor pointed to the outside where the cries of battle rose and fell and carried across every room.

"Yes, I hear it!" Idalia's eyes flashed, "It's the sound of your mistakes. Those are *your* men doing this."

"Then tell me why *his* men were so readily prepared to fight back?" Trevor reasoned, and Idalia hated that he was standing in such a sacred space while defiling the name of her Prince.

"Did you expect them to lie down and die? Of course they would fight back!" Idalia stalked towards her husband.

"You look different again." Was his reply.

Idalia's jaw dropped in a dumbfounded expression.

"You're not serious. *That's* what you're worried about?"

Trevor shrugged one shoulder, raising the lantern he held. "It was just an observation." He exhaled and looked around the oasis. "This is quite nice, all things considered."

Idalia didn't like the look in his eye. Malicious, with a tinge of vengefulness. "I'm going to ask you again, what are you doing here?"

Trevor dug the toe of his boot into a delicate violet, crushing it. "To get you, of course." He gave her an exasperated expression. "Something about a marital plead, and the soldiers were ready to strike. So it seemed like a good deal."

A good deal. That was what her life amounted to in his head.

"I need you to call your soldiers off, this is bigger than either of us. You don't understand-"

"No, Idalia. I think I understand perfectly. You love that creature. You're willing to betray all of us, to protect him. Tell me if I'm getting warmer." Trevor looked nastier than she'd ever seen him. Or perhaps, he always had been, and she'd been too trusting to notice.

"Yes, Trevor. I love him. But I also love my people, and if we don't stop this, you can say you had a hand in their annihilation."

Another shrug, "It's for the greater good. Something that I think you've yet to grasp."

Idalia's shoulders stiffened, and her anger fueled her words. "I spent so long," she took a step towards him, and then another, "waiting for you all to see me as someone who was like you." A scoff fell from her lips. "But do you know what? I would rather die than be compared to you." Without even realizing it, Idalia had raised her sword towards Trevor's chest.

Trevor's features morphed yet again, as if he hadn't expected her to act on her words. But she would. She was a soldier, stronger than him in ways that he could never dream of.

"Then it looks like you won't need me to plead for you after all." He spat and lifted the flickering lantern towards the rocky wall. When his intent became clear, Idalia's anger started to wink out. "Don't." She ordered.

"Throw your sword." Trevor countered, watching her with a pointed gaze.

Idalia's grip faltered along the handle of her blade, and the lantern started swinging slightly.

"Fine." She tossed the steel to her right, and it landed soundlessly amongst the blanket of grass.

Trevor's shoulders relaxed and his face softened. "I wish I could have protected your naivety, Dilly-Dally." He sighed, before he swung his arm and slammed the lantern into the rock.

"No!" Idalia yelled, throwing herself in Trevor's direction. The glass shattered immediately upon impact, and the flames started to lick up everything in their wake. The trees that had curved to form archways turned into pillars of fire. The heavy odor of smoke and burnt flowers flooded the atmosphere as Idalia slammed Trevor into the ground. "Why would you do that?" She shouted.

"They don't deserve any beauty." He retorted as he struggled to get out from underneath her. "You fit here."

At one point in time, those words would have stabbed Idalia to her very core, but now, they made her lips pull back in a vicious smile as she struck Trevor on the side of his head.

"You're right, Trevor. I do."

Chapter Fifty
The Decision

Idalia rose to her feet, leaving Trevor's limp silhouette to collect ash as she painfully took in the damage that he had caused. Sylvie's oasis, once green and beautiful, was now engulfed in flames and destruction. Idalia couldn't even hear the rush of the waterfall over the sound of crackling fire. "I'm so sorry, Sylvie." Idalia uttered under her breath. She didn't allow herself a moment to reflect on each sweet memory that she had collected with Erin in this space. She only stooped to gather her abandoned sword and to press a kiss to her hand to place on the doorway as she shut the door. Idalia didn't see the flames that licked underneath it, like angry molten fingers desperately trying to claw their way out into the open.

More smoke. Idalia's head whipped around as she saw billows of gray filling the corridors to her left. *Someone had started another fire.*

Idalia covered her mouth and nose with her sleeve and started towards the rapidly darkening hallway. Before she could cross the threshold, a blonde woman covered from head to toe in scuffed black leather stalked out with the smoke curling at her ankles as if she herself could command it. The woman cocked her head and sized Idalia up.

"Servant, slave or prisoner?" She asked, dragging the tip of her sword around the floor in a lazy semi-circle with a small motion of her wrist.

"Why does it matter?" Idalia kept her features composed, she had yet to meet a soldier who didn't immediately lunge at her, but her mind chanted three different options. *Daughter, fiancée, widow.*

The female raised her eyebrow, "Good, always question authority." Then she shifted her grip on her sword and thrust it at Idalia.

Idalia threw her weight to her side, narrowly dodging the attack. "Gate or Esterod?" Idalia quipped, swinging her own sword to clash with the other woman's. Sparks bounced carelessly from their metal and Idalia couldn't help but wonder if that was the cause of the other fire.

The woman's pale lips pulled back to reveal perfect, white teeth. "Why does it matter?" She parroted and dropped down to knock Idalia's balance out from under her. Idalia saw the move coming and jumped over the woman's swinging leg.

"Because I don't want to fight either one." Idalia panted, dancing on the balls of her feet as she tried to determine what the woman's next move would be.

"You're definitely not a servant." The blonde blew a lock of hair away that had loosed itself from her messy braid and their swords collided once again in a storm of metal and adrenaline.

"How'd you draw that conclusion?" Idalia leapt backward as the woman swung her blade low.

"All the ones I've seen tonight practically drip fear. You're a fighter."

Idalia lifted the hilt of her sword pointedly towards the blonde. "This war is unnecessary."

The woman's lips curled into a smirk, "Probably, but it's fun." With that, the woman let her sword slip from her hand to crash onto the marble. She moved in a slow circle around Idalia.

Idalia would have thought that it was absurd to be left weaponless when one's opponent still held a sizable blade, but this woman gave off the impression that her deadliness was not restricted only to how she wielded a sword.

"How is war ever fun?" Idalia kept her knees slightly bent just in case she needed to leap out of the way on a milliseconds notice.

"Because we usually win." The woman smiled almost haughtily, before ceasing her circular prowling. "So tell me, what side are you on?"

Idalia watched the blonde with a wary gaze as she slowly retracted her sword. "The side I should have been on years ago. The one that doesn't end in this madness."

The woman surveyed Idalia and to her shock, extended a calloused hand coated in a fingerless glove. "While it's less fun, I will admit I thought that all this was a bit... much." The woman tilted her head, causing her braid to slip over her leather-clad shoulder.

Relief coursed through Idalia's veins, running alongside her adrenaline. "Do you have a name?"

"Majele." She gave Idalia a smile that was all teeth. The woman had a feral sort of beauty encompassing her. A sense of wild unpredictability that could prove to be incredibly useful or exceedingly treacherous. "What do you say? Truce?"

Idalia shook Majele's hand. "The only way to stop this war is to cut out its heart." She stated as they quickened their pace down the smoke-encroached hallway.

"I can get behind that." Majele flashed a grin as she plucked a dagger from her waist.

The would-have-been Princess of the Gate and an Author-sent Esterod soldier walked with synchronized intent towards a common target.

Idalia could only pray that they weren't too late.

Chapter Fifty-One
The Culmination

"So which one am I not allowed to kill?" Majele questioned as their feet pounded the marble.

"The one in white, it's his brother that's the problem." Idalia lifted her hand to signal their immediate need to halt.

The large double doors to the lavish dining room were cracked open, and the clashing of swords emanated from within. Idalia craned her neck to peer into the space. Eight guards were sprawled like ragdolls in various positions across the floor. Two abnormally large men with an assortment of knives strapped across their chests were placed on either side of Lester and Erin stood in front. His chest was heaving from the exertion and yet Lester seemed as collected as ever.

How strange, Idalia thought. For how much Lester delights in bloodshed, he made no moves to strangle his brother himself. Then it hit her. It was never about the blood on his hands. To Lester it was about the amount of power that he could leech from others and right now, Erin was powerless against him. Lester was reveling in the knowledge that he'd finally succeeded against the only person who ever posed a threat to him. Idalia gritted her teeth. *That just won't do.*

There was one benefit that she gleaned from being around the evil Prince. She had gotten very good at reading his tells. The instant that Lester's lips curled with the promise of breaking his brother further, Idalia nodded to Majele, and they thrust the gilded doors open as a calvary of two. Lester loosed a petulant sigh. "The both of you never learn." He snapped his ringed fingers and the massive guards sprung on them. Erin shot Idalia a questioning look. *Can you handle them?*

Idalia offered the slightest tilt of her chin. *Let's end this.* As those three words were conveyed with a single flick of her eyes, Idalia went to battle against a stranger. Erin went to war against his blood.

Idalia had attended many balls as a guest here, but fighting was a dance all its own. A rhythmic movement where one wrong stance could cost you your life, but the right steps well executed could save it. The guard that Idalia was up against was undoubtedly stronger, but she was lithe.

To Idalia's left, Majele cut down her opponent as if he was a large tree in need of pruning. She grinned while she did so, and the fact that this woman enjoyed it so much should have sent a shiver down Idalia's spine. However, she couldn't have been more grateful. Idalia's boots squelched from the landing that came with her backwards leap. She tried not to think about whose blood fused itself to the soles of her shoes, but it did make her footing slick as her adversary swung at her in full force. Idalia tried to escape the punch, but the man's fist connected with her gut in her attempt to steady her footing. Idalia dropped to her knees, bruising them on the stone surface as breath violently expelled itself from her lungs. The man kicked her sword to the side where it collided with a marble pillar. *She couldn't think.* The combination of pain blooming across her stomach and the near certain sensation that she would vomit was all the guard needed to hurl several knives in her direction. She gulped down whatever air she could and rolled to the side, staining her clothes in the spreading carmine pools. Her mind slowly started to lose its fogginess and her ears roared with the intense volume of warring steel and clattering knives. Idalia pushed herself up onto her elbows and reached for one of the offending daggers that lay haphazardly amongst a sea of black and burgundy. The blade wouldn't be long enough to pierce through his armor even if the guard continued to advance upon her. She needed to retrieve her sword.

With a heavy grunt, Majele's combatant collapsed with her blade wedged in between his midsection and his chest plate. She drew it out, tossed her fraying braid over her shoulder and without missing a beat, swung for the guard who roughly latched onto Idalia's leg as she edged towards her sword.

"You're annoying both of us." She snarled, and jumped onto the man's back as she twisted her waist-length braid around his neck. She yanked backwards on the makeshift rope and the guard's eyes bulged as he clawed at her and tried to buck her off like an angry bull. Majele clamped her thighs around his neck and locked her ankles to stay upright until the guard's aggressive motions started to wane and Idalia watched his lips turn an alarming shade of purple.

Seeing that Majele had the situation handled, Idalia sprung for her sword and turned her attention to her

Prince. Fresh blood trickled out of a slash on Erin's shoulder, spreading across his shirt like rose petals unfurling. Lester's bottom lip was split open with a cut that trailed down his chin, more than likely slit by the prongs on one of Erin's rings. Lester had a white-knuckled grip on his blade, and feigned striking Erin's head when in reality, his heavy boot propelled itself into Erin's broken ribs. A gut-wrenching groan slipped from his lips and he doubled over in pain. Lester dragged his knuckles over his lips that twisted in triumph as he strode towards Erin.

Idalia crept towards the dining table on silent feet. *Hold on, Erin.* Lester gave a breathy chuckle as he savored Erin's winces of agony and tilted his brother's chin up with the point of his stained sword. "You should have stayed down."

"You rule over a kingdom of glass." Erin rasped as a trickle of crimson flowed underneath his chin when Lester pressed his blade into the sensitive skin.

"Oh, my dear brother, glass can *slice*."

Erin's caramel eyes glanced up and over Lester's shoulder before a slow smile pulled his lips back from his teeth. "You're right."

Lester raised an eyebrow and made the mistake of looking over his shoulder. Idalia towered over the both of them as she stood firmly planted on the mahogany surface.

"Don't touch my family." She seethed and smashed the wine bottle she had swiped from the table over Lester's head. Shards of opaque glass sprayed in all directions and Lester landed amongst them.

"That's my girl." Erin said with a mixture of pride and pain in his expression as she jumped down from the table and helped him to his feet. He faltered, as a throbbing ache shot up his side and his knees nearly buckled.

"I've got you." Idalia grunted as she shouldered his weight. The tinkling of glass shards shuffled under her, and Idalia was suddenly painfully aware of a fierce rip in her skin that seized her leg. Warm, scarlet, blood poured over the curve of her calf around a jagged fragment of glass that Lester had just managed to imbed in her leg. Erin's gaze turned murderous as Lester chuckled and rose to his feet.

Idalia inhaled sharply and tucked herself behind Erin. His hand reached backwards to her, perhaps in an attempt to ease her pain as well as his.

"You two deserve each other. I'll put your graves side by side." A malicious sneer crossed his face as he plucked slivers of glass from his palms. Then he lunged. And the Prince of the Gate was impaled by a dagger.

Chapter Fifty-Two
We Burn Together

Lester's eyes bore holes into their heads before his gaze tracked downwards to the ornate dagger handle protruding from his chest. Flecks of blood had sprayed Erin's hand as he gripped the hilt. When Erin had reached his hand behind his back to Idalia, she had passed him one of the throwing knives that she'd collected from that guard. They only had a heartbeat to make the exchange before Lester thrust his body forward.

"It's over." Erin tightened his jaw as the dagger pushed even further into his brother's sternum. Lester sank heavily to his knees before toppling over onto his back, the dagger glinting in the torchlight like a gory decoration.

The serpent smiled, which was a foul sight with his blood bubbling up through his lips and spilling over his words. "It's already done." He croaked as his blackened soul departed from his body. Lester's eyes looked to the ceiling, never to blink again.

Erin's grasp slipped from the knife, and his shallow breaths slowly evened out into something deeper. Idalia limped to his side to press a reassuring hand to his forearm.

"You're free." She whispered, and Erin's eyes locked with hers.

"Not yet." A grave expression washed over his features as he took several steps back from the lifeless body of his brother.

"Guys, we have a problem." Majele called as she strode towards the dining room doors, and in that moment Idalia realized that the air around them had a certain haze to it and a thick, ashy aroma. The fire was spreading.

"We don't know how widespread the flames are, if there are any soldiers that are still alive we need to get them out." Idalia stated.

Majele agreed, "And I guess it doesn't matter if they're Gate or Esterod?"

Both Erin and Idalia shook their heads simultaneously.

"If they're alive, get them outside." Erin instructed, and Majele adjusted her hold on the handle of her blade before she left to carry out the task. Idalia couldn't help but wonder if the soldiers that Majele encountered would be forced to cooperate simply because she threatened them.

Erin retrieved his own sword and held his hand out to Idalia.

"Thank you." He murmured.

"This is my home too." Idalia touched his cheek. The hopes she held for their future once soared and then plummeted. Now, she could feel them precariously balance on a thin thread that could be so easily snapped as the next events unfurled.

Even in the midst of possible destruction, Erin and Idalia would not hesitate to save any lives at risk. The palace was burning, the Gate was open, and its Prince was dead. Those three factors would either end this war or fuel it.

So, they joined their hands and stepped into the fire.

The Murmur

I never understood how time could control a life until I met her. It is constant. It is fleeting. It is priceless. No matter how hard I tried, I couldn't force it to stop. No amount of power will buy a person more of it.

Still, that hasn't stopped me from using up every last wish over this past year for five more minutes.

There was so much I wanted to say.

Chapter Fifty-Three
What We Still Have to Lose

F resh waves of blazing heat rolled through the air as Idalia sank to her knees to check the pulse of an unconscious man. The scent of smoke clung to her skin. It didn't dissipate no matter how many trips they made out into the open air as they hauled limp soldiers away from the leaping flames. She was convinced that the marble flooring would be forever tainted by the blood that had been spilled. *For what? There was no winner in this war, just families that would be missing one spot at their table.*

She covered her mouth with her dingy sleeve and refused to give into the tingling in the back of her throat. Her vision was already hazy with all the smoke making her eyes water. The heartbeat of the wounded soldier that Idalia felt weakly tremor underneath her fingers, slipped away like ice in the sun. To her left, Erin shook his head.

"They're gone." He coughed, and the motion jarred his ribs. He ended up drawing in a larger, smoke-filled breath from the pain instead of expelling one.

"No one was in the prison besides us, right?" Idalia stepped over the armored bodies. She wished that it had never come to this, but it wasn't over yet.

"No, but that's the next place we need to check." Erin reached for her arm, and they made their way towards the cavernous staircase. Idalia didn't even register the stench that she usually associated with the prison. She only smelled ash and blood and felt the dwindling seconds. The heaviness in the air lessened with each step downwards. How much worse would this have been if they hadn't gotten all the captives across? Idalia's stomach lurched as their feet struck the final stair. There were bodies here, but they weren't Esterod soldiers. Idalia recognized five of the seven men who had once sworn an oath to them, now lying in horribly contorted positions. Two of them were gutted, and the darkening pool underneath their bodies spread and settled into every crevice and crack of the soiled floor.

The grim image before them worsened when Idalia noticed that each victim's shoulder was covered with the same type of cloth. "There's a symbol on this." Erin said gravely.

A wave of nausea racked through her body as she forced herself to look closer. A hibiscus, with a sword for a stem. A Sentry patch. "They killed them." She whispered. Idalia was met with a flash of memory of that precious night in the refuge. She heard the voice of that little girl who praised Erin for saving her father from the 'bad men.'

Idalia had known something wasn't right at that moment, but perhaps she didn't fully grasp how twisted the minds of Thultan's presumed saviors were. She was disgusted to have ever called herself one of them. As they ran up the stairwell, Idalia couldn't help but imagine that the same men who she had once dragged home from the Tap were capable of such gory murder. The line between good and evil was just that, a line. One that's just as easy to walk alongside as it is to cross.

"I've only found three that were still breathing in the west wing." Majele's strong voice floated to their ears along with bits and pieces of burning wallpaper carried by an unseen current. "I lugged them outside." She added, before she dashed towards the other wing.

"We can get buckets and try to put out what we can from the waterfall." Erin started to turn on his heel towards Sylvie's Oasis, and it pained Idalia to have to stop him.

"We can't. I'm sorry Erin, it's too late. Trevor got to it first, but he's gone now." Her fingers grasped his sleeve, and Idalia knew that his eyes weren't only glassy because of the smoke. Then she watched that gaze trail over her shoulder and land on something behind her.

Calliope was the last thing that Idalia expected to see when she rotated her body.

Chapter Fifty-Four
Back From the Dead

"Erin, it's been a while." Calliope prowled towards them with a stillness that seemed inhuman, as if she could glide across the floor without bending a knee.

"Let me guess, takeover gone wrong?" Her eyes locked onto Erin and dragged her gaze over his body before it locked onto the bloody stain at his shoulder. "You always were prettier than your brother." She cooed.

Idalia edged closer to Erin, and she could feel the tension radiating from the muscles in his arm. Calliope's eyes shot to her. Gooseflesh rippled over Idalia's skin at the vast pools of an inky wasteland that was the other woman's eyes. *Weren't they green before?*

A dissatisfied expression twisted her features, enhancing the deep cavity-like hollows in her cheeks. "Oh, that's right. You're the reason she died." Calliope muttered thoughtfully.

"Why are you here?" Idalia held her head higher.

"Aw, pet." Calliope's voice held all the sickening sweetness of cobra venom. "I never left." She cocked her head, causing oily hair to slither behind her shoulder. "And neither did he." She raised a bony finger behind Erin and Idalia.

"Matthias." Hesitation laced Erin's voice, and the hair stood up on the back of Idalia's neck at the smile that the prisoner she had once befriended gave. It was too wide, too unfeeling. An alarming grin and a destructive gaze.

"Not the reunion you were hoping for?" He cracked his neck. "Shouldn't have been so trusting, Shifter-boy."

Erin and Idalia had a fraction of a second to share a darting glance.

"So it was an act, the entire time?" Erin broke away from Idalia to lead the much larger man's attention away from her. "You wanted a second chance." He walked with the certainty of one whose ribs were still unshattered, but Idalia wasn't sure how long he'd be able to keep up that ruse.

Matthias chuckled deep in his throat, "I lied." He deftly twisted a razor-sharp knife between his fingers. "I'm quite good at it." His eyes tracked to Erin's side that he was quite literally holding together. "But that's not the only thing

I'm good at." A ghost of a malevolent smile crossed his lips before he lunged in Erin's direction. Erin sidestepped Matthias's hurtling mass and out of the corner of Idalia's eye, she saw both men draw their blades.

"You've been a thorn in my side since you showed up," Calliope hissed. The sharp comment diverted Idalia's attention.

"Why didn't you get out when you could?" Idalia took several, slow steps backwards. They would need space for the scrimmage that seemed inevitable. However, for each step that Idalia purposely retreated, Calliope advanced.

"I tried." A dark laugh bubbled over her lips. "I did everything right, too." She popped her knuckles at her side with a force that could have snapped the bones.

"I got the royal puppet over there to change me. I was *this* close," she pinched her thumb and forefinger together so harshly that the skin went white, "to leaving, but then the disguise fell." Calliope brandished two knives from her pockets. "You *ruined* me." Her voice sounded curdled, and *wrong*.

"I did nothing to you." Idalia said steadily, inching her fingers around the hilt of her sword for a better grip. She couldn't tell where Calliope's pupils ended, and her iris began. The thought was as unsettling as the sensation of sticky blood that still poured from Idalia's calf and leeched into her shoes.

"You killed me." Calliope growled, then she seemed to reconsider. "Actually, you made me better."

"I'm not sure I follow." Idalia refrained from coughing as more smoke filled her nostrils.

"I'm not weak, anymore." She snarled and flung her body in an arc towards Idalia. The velocity sent them both to the ground and Calliope dug her fingernails into Idalia's skin as they rolled. Idalia slammed the heel of her hand upwards towards Calliope's chin, and the resounding sound of her upper and lower jaw violently clacking together echoed through the room and bounced off the pillars.

Her eyes snapped to Idalia, and she spat out a mouthful of blood that leaked from her punctured tongue. A trickle of crimson dribbled down her chin as an unhinged gleam sparked in her coal-dark eyes. An almost feral screech of anger tore from Calliope's throat, and she slammed Idalia's wrist into the marble, eliciting a grunt of pain from the would-have-been Princess. Calliope towered on top of Idalia, and her hands flew towards Idalia's throat. Before they could latch on, Idalia pushed her knees up into the other woman's stomach. She coughed, the smoky air a poor replacement for the oxygen that her lungs needed to replace. Idalia pulled herself to her feet and snatched her sword, holding the blade from her midsection as a barrier between her body and her enraged opponent.

"Fine, let's play with knives." Calliope plucked her scattered daggers from the floor, and she hurtled towards Idalia. Idalia was exhausted, and her limbs were starting to expel less and less energy as her body tried to compensate for the blood that she was losing. Idalia's sluggishness gave Calliope an opening to slash her stomach. She gasped and pressed her hand to the wound. It wasn't deep, but the shock of the sting forced adrenaline-created stamina to flood Idalia's body. She wasn't sure how long it would last.

Idalia grasped Calliope's wrist and wrenched it at a painfully contorted angle. The woman grunted and one of her daggers slipped to the floor before she drove her knee into Idalia's sliced stomach. It felt like a ton of bricks collapsed onto Idalia's chest as her lungs compressed. *This wasn't it; she wouldn't allow this to be her end.* As the heels of Idalia's hands struck the marble to catch her body, Calliope grabbed Idalia's calf. A cry of searing pain flew from her throat as her attacker twisted the shard of glass even further into the throbbing flesh. For a moment, the lashing sensation stole away her ability to think as fresh, hot blood gushed from the wound, coating the floor in red.

Idalia clamped down on her tongue, willing the sharp jab of her incisors to distract her body from the stabbing agony of her leg as she swiped her blade towards Calliope's ankles. She leapt in reverse and lost her balance as her foot came down on the arm of a perished soldier that sent Calliope backwards. The air had only slowly started to filter through Idalia's lungs once more before Calliope was back on her feet with a white-knuckled grip on a sword that she'd stolen from the body of a fallen soldier.

Both women thrust their weight towards each other, blades swinging. "You know what's different about us?" Calliope said between pants for air, "I had the guts to do things you never would have."

Idalia's muscles burned as she forced her sword to counter Calliope's blade. "And look where that got you." Idalia reared her hand back and struck Calliope across the face, leaving the dark-eyed woman to reel in her momentary disorientation. Calliope seethed and dragged her knuckles over her bruising jaw. She ignored the thick blood that gushed from her nostril and roared, "I'm going to carve your heart out!" Calliope shifted her weight to her back foot and thrust her leg towards Idalia's sword. The blade flew free of Idalia's grasp and clattered against a pillar. She wouldn't reach it in time. Idalia called on every ounce of energy that she had left and forced her limbs to carry her to the wall. It was agonizing to run, as every step jolted that shard of glass in her calf and her body begged for a reprieve. But a reprieve would give Calliope an opportunity to act upon her heart-carving promise. So, Idalia's nails latched onto the rope that tied the drapes back from the fogging glass and pulled it free.

Calliope laughed darkly, "A curtain tie, I'm terrified." She snarled and sliced through the thick air as her unrelenting steel found its mark.

Or so she thought, but Idalia had chosen that split second to dive to the side. Her elbow sang with the ache of bone against stone as she landed. Calliope flashed Idalia a ferocious display of teeth as she struggled to pull her sword from its wedged position in the window casing. Idalia took two steps back, wrapping a bit of the cord around her hand. The woman's abyss-like gaze darted to the braided cable.

"Please do hang yourself with it."

"Oh this isn't for me." Idalia pushed her hair back from her beaded forehead and hurtled behind Calliope as she pulled the cord around the woman's throat. Calliope staggered back with a choking gasp, and her hands flew from the hilt of her lodged sword to claw at her throat. Idalia wrenched the cable taut against Calliope's windpipe.

Calliope gagged and writhed, before her knuckles flew back to strike Idalia close to her temple. The blow weakened Idalia's strangling efforts and Calliope hurled her body backward. She was going to crush Idalia when they landed.

Matthias bared his teeth as he thrust his fist at Erin's jaw, leaving a darkening purple bruise as the Prince's head reeled back and his teeth vibrated from the impact. Erin dropped into a crouching position before Matthias could strike again. Erin then lunged at the other man's waist, pinning him to the floor.

"You don't have to do this, Matthias." Erin panted, "This isn't you."

Matthias spat on him. "I'm not caged anymore." He shoved the palms of his hands into Erin's chest, pushing him away. "This is for what he's done." His gaze darkened into a plunging pool of crude oil as he snatched his sword and leapt to his feet before hurling it down towards Erin's body.

Erin scrambled for his own weapon and narrowly avoided the loss of his right arm as their blades crashed together. "I'm not my brother." He grunted as Matthias exerted more pressure into his blade and deep, rolling pangs of excruciating pain spread through Erin's side like a million stabbing daggers.

"It's the same blood." Matthias grumbled, shifting his balance to his other foot. "And I want to spill it."

Erin clamped down on a pained groan and thrust his legs up to knock Matthias flat against the floor. The other man's body landed with a thud, and his sword skittered out of his reach. As Erin was about to lunge for Matthias before he could regain his bearings, a gurgling wheeze filled his ears. His gaze shot to Calliope struggling against Idalia with the tenacity of a rabid mountain lion. Suddenly, Calliope lurched backwards with the clear intent to take his Jewel down with her.

However, when Idalia's body met the ground she was not pinned underneath the weight of her attacker, because a blur of movement viciously yanked Calliope to the marble.

Chapter Fifty-Five

Her Final Stand

Erin then slammed Calliope into the wall. "Don't you *ever* touch her again."

"Who would listen to you?" Calliope bared her teeth and directed her force towards his ribs which extracted another crack from his side. Idalia saw him wrench his eyes shut for a mere second before he pinned Calliope's arms to either side of her. She tried to kick Erin's balance out from underneath him. But before Idalia could tell if she succeeded or not, Matthias smacked the wall in aggravation and pushed himself upright. His hair hung limply in his face as he rose to his full height.

Across from them, Erin seethed. "Lester won't come for you, he's dead." and Calliope's blood-stained teeth gleamed in the ashy haze.

"Good." Her vile tone momentarily stole Idalia's focus but when she looked back, Matthias was gone.

A torrent of unease crawled over Idalia's spine, and she raised her sword. *This wasn't right.*

Her senses were clouded by the smoke and exhaustion, so she was blind to the shadow that crept up behind her on soundless feet. Suddenly, a rough, cold hand wrapped around her throat and the other clamped over her mouth before she could scream.

"It's already done." Matthias snarled in her ear and Idalia felt her feet drag underneath her despite how desperately she tried to wrench her body away from his vice-like grip. *Lester had said that.* Idalia's mind started to panic. She clamped down on the fingers that smothered her mouth as harshly as her jaw would allow. When Matthias yanked his throbbing hand from her face, She yelled for Erin.

Idalia's plea didn't reach the Prince's ears in time. With a growl, Erin drove Calliope's own sword into her heart. His chest heaved as he turned around at the very instant that Matthias grabbed Idalia's shoulders and rammed her body into a marble pillar. A sickening crack resounded through the air and a scream tore from his throat. The horrible snap echoed until the very vibration of it was etched into Erin's mind. Matthias backed away from her crumpled body and the pool of blood that spread from underneath her.

Idalia was gone.

One Year Later

Epilogue: Upside-Down Roses

The King of the Gate never missed a visit. He would sit down on the well-worn chaise at her bedside and recount memories. He would weave them together, starting at the beginning and always promising to continue tomorrow. Then the tomorrows began to accumulate until a year had gone by.

The girl that he spoke to was always quiet, always still. She didn't interject with her own version of the story, but she would listen. She never opened her eyes to see the face of her storyteller.

She would listen for as long as the King would talk. After all, he promised that he would never say goodbye.

The girl lay as peaceful as a doll in a bed of white, with roses curling from the swooping iron bedposts and their burgundy petals fluttering down to caress her unfeeling cheek.

The King would hold her hand on days that she went as still as death. He told her stories, and sometimes the girl heard bits and pieces of his voice murmur to her in the darkness.

Other times, she heard nothing at all.

The Murmur

This is where our story comes to a close my love. Although I will never tire of telling it to you, it is time for you to come back to me. Our dreams are only beginning. Wake up.

Acknowledgements

Before I thank any one person, I must thank the Author. My Creator who has enabled me to pursue this dream and who has shown His guiding hand in my life in more ways than I can count. Next, the biggest thank you goes to my parents. Mom and Dad, I would not be who I am today without you both. I couldn't be more grateful for your wisdom and instruction and the love that I have felt follow me throughout my life.

Mama, words cannot express just how much your support and love has meant to me throughout my entire life. You have always been my rock, my comfort, and my sunshine. I will forever treasure all of the memories that we share. I couldn't have asked for a more loving mother, thank you for everything. I'm quite sure that you've memorized this book inside and out, and I love how you rooted for Erin and Idalia from the beginning. You were such a wonderful editor, and I will forever treasure the inside jokes that came with this adventure. Thank you for always being my biggest cheerleader from day one and supporting me through each step of my life, including this new chapter. Mama, I can't contain all the love I have for you. There's no way I could do this without you.

Dad, your constant support and encouragement has meant the world to me. You have been an amazing father. I truly couldn't have hand-picked a better dad. I will forever cherish all of our wonderful memories. Thank you for always standing by me and being there for me. I am so thankful to you for modeling what a true man of honesty and integrity looks like. I am so blessed to be your daughter. It means so much to me that you have lovingly supported my dreams. I will always remember the fun that we had throughout this journey. I love you so much Dad.

For my family, you guys have been such wonderful cheerleaders throughout this process and it means so much to me. I'm so blessed to have you in my corner, and thank you for the encouragement and all the laughs. You will always have the first looks into my new novels, and I can't wait to share this journey with you.

And last but never least, a huge thank you to my amazing readers! I am overwhelmed with the amount of support and excitement that When You Return recieved, and I hope that you loved Erin and Idalia's story as much as I did. Thank you for allowing me to share this chapter of my life with you. I can't wait to see what the future holds.

About the Author

Isabella Ayubi has been a lover of literature since she was a child. In her spare time, you can always find her curled up with a good book, or with a pencil and sketchbook in hand as she draws the fantastical images that stem from her imagination. One of her dreams is to have a home library with a rolling ladder, where she can be surrounded by beautiful works of literature as she writes her future novels. If you want to talk bookish things, you can find her on Instagram, @authorisabellaayubi, or her website, www.authorisabellaayubi.com.

Milton Keynes UK
Ingram Content Group UK Ltd.
UKHW051844210424
441487UK00016B/92/J

9 798989 901623